OUT OF BOUNDS

Brit Boys Sports Romance

J.H. CROIX

J.H. CROIX

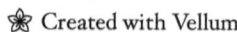 Created with Vellum

To DBC. All ways. Always.

Chapter One

ETHAN

A fist glanced off the side of my chin, and I reflexively swung back. I shan't say I meant to clock the guy right on the nose, but then I'd walked right into this fight. Literally. Blood streaked down the guy's chin while he kept swinging, swearing a mile a minute while he was at it. I managed to dodge another fist and slip out of the midst of the scuffle. It was in the wee hours of the morning, and I'd meant to just skip out of the bar where I'd gone with a few mates from my football team. I hadn't been paying much attention and, truth be told, I was a tad sloshed from a few too many beers. I wasn't prone to drink much as a rule, so when I did, I tended to get fuzzy fast. Hence, I'd been making my way outside and didn't even notice the guys in the middle of a heated argument.

A quick scan around, and I deduced I'd slipped my way clear. Last thing I wanted was Coach to find out I'd stumbled into a fight, so I headed outside into the rainy Seattle darkness. I tugged the hood from my jacket up and turned to walk to my flat when I heard my name. "Ethan Walsh?"

I turned back to see a police officer standing beside one of the bartenders. Bloody hell. I nodded politely. "Yes, sir."

I might have just accidentally punched someone, but I had manners. Fat lot of good they did me. Before I knew it, I'd been bundled into the officer's car and watched while another officer stuffed the two guys whose fight it had actually been into another car. The officer who seemed to be in charge of me was friendly enough.

"Mr. Walsh, as far as I understand, you happened to be in the wrong place at the wrong time. Problem is, the guy you hit is pretty upset about the whole thing and drunk to boot, so he's not listening to reason. We'll get to the station and sort this out. There were plenty of witnesses who report you walked right through and took one on the jaw first."

The officer jabbered on a bit, while I put my face in my hands and sighed. Great, fucking great. I don't know how long it was until we arrived at the station, but I immediately declared I needed to talk to someone. Friendly though the officers were, the arse whose fist bounced off my face was none too happy about his bloody nose. I made quick call to Tristan, my flat mate who'd had enough sense not to be out at the bar tonight. He chuckled and assured me he'd call Coach and get someone from the team sent my way.

I was a player for the Seattle Stars, a US football team spending big bucks to sign footballers from all over the world. Correction: soccer team. There were many bits I'd come to love about America, but their silly idea to call another sport—an inferior one I don't mind saying—football was a constant irritation. The rest of the whole wide world of sports called football *football*, but in the US it was soccer, or no one knew what you meant. Anyway, hard to believe it but I was an elite player and had lucked into this team after a solid pro start back in Britain. Downside to all this meant it wouldn't be too great for me to make a ruckus for my team. Our Coach—whom I respected, I truly did—had little tolerance for players getting into silly messes.

I leaned my chin in my hand and waited. They'd deposited me in a room that didn't have much of anything in it, other than a table and a phone. I don't know how long I waited, but out of the dead silence in the room came a sharp knock. Before I managed to fully stand, the door swung open. I almost knocked my chair over when I saw Zoe Lawson in the doorway

Zoe stepped into the room, closed the door behind her and walked briskly to the table, sitting down and eyeing me. "Hello Ethan," she said.

I sat down and bit back the sigh that wanted to escape. Zoe Lawson was a criminal defense attorney I'd met a bit ago when she helped Alex Gordon with his assault charges after he hauled off and punched the asshole who'd raped his girlfriend a few years prior. Alex was one of my mates from Britain and the goalkeeper for the Stars. Alex, being Alex, had assault charges for a hella good reason. Me, well, I didn't even know if I was charged with anything yet, but all I'd done was basically walk into someone's fist and react.

Now, here was Zoe. Zoe was, well, she was flat beautiful. I don't know if she was the most beautiful woman ever, but she was to me. She was also slightly terrifying. She stood close to six feet tall with legs that went on forever. Although she must've rolled out of bed to come meet with me, she looked tidy and professional in a navy jacket over a fitted skirt that fell to her knees. Her auburn hair was pulled back into a sleek knot, not a single tendril escaping. Her gorgeous hair was paired with hazel eyes and fair skin. The only thing that softened her was her face—she had a wide, full mouth, eyes that tilted at the corners and rosy cheeks.

Oh, and the last time I saw her, I'd kissed her. I'd encountered her by chance when I was leaving a restaurant. I'd had a few beers and didn't give a damn about her stand-offish attitude at that moment. I'd taken full advantage of how surprised she looked when she saw me and just kissed her right there in the hallway of the restaurant. For a flash, her mouth had softened and she'd arched into me. Sanity must've hit her, but not before our tongues did a quick dance. Definitely not before I'd felt every inch of her flush against me. That brief taste had ended with her shoving me away and glaring at me before she stalked off. I hadn't seen her since.

I looked across the table and felt caught between impulses. On the one hand, I wanted to walk around the table between us and untie her hair. I'd fantasized a few times about what that gorgeous hair might look like loose, but all I could do was imagine. The unflattering fluorescent lights couldn't even dim its brightness, streaks of gold winked out amidst the rich auburn.

On the other hand, I felt a bit foolish. The hands of the simple black and white clock on the wall above the door told me it was approaching one-thirty in the morning now. I didn't have a good explanation for why I'd ended up in this little mess, but here I was, wondering how to explain myself to Zoe.

Bloody hell. Zoe Lawson commanded any room she stepped into. She exuded brilliance and confidence and wasn't the slightest bit intimidated. It was no wonder I wanted her like mad.

I didn't realize I was just sitting there like a dolt until Zoe drummed her fingers on the desk.

"Can you handle a simple hello?" she asked, a tad sharply.

Oh, that did it. I straightened and eyed her.

"Hello Zoe. What brings you here this evening?" I asked, leaning heavy on the haughty in my tone.

Zoe arched a brow and leaned back in her chair. "It's morning Ethan, and you apparently managed to get yourself in a little fix. Coach Hoffman called and asked me to come meet with you." She paused and glanced pointedly at her watch. "At 1:30am." Her gorgeous hazel eyes—layers of green and nutmeg swirled together with flecks of gold—lifted to mine again. Her gaze ensnared me, and she had to clear her throat to snap me back to attention.

"Aye, I suppose it's a bit late, or early, depending on how you look at it," I finally managed.

She inclined her head slightly and pulled a small notebook out of her purse. "Tell me what happened."

I quickly summarized and couldn't help but grin when her lips twitched. I wasn't grinning because any of it was funny. No, rather I loved getting under her skin like I had with that kiss. It wasn't easy though. I had to credit her there. But the corner of her mouth curled up, just the slightest bit, and I loved it. Blood shot straight to my groin.

Pay attention, mate. Not the time to get all randy.

"Ethan, tell it to me straight. Did you really walk right into the middle of a fight? Because I'll be honest, it sounds a bit ridiculous."

I eyed her, thinking I didn't really want to keep talking about this. I knew it sounded bloody ridiculous, but it was the truth.

Chapter Two

ZOE

Ethan Walsh looked over at me with a half-grin and a shrug. Even a half-grin from him was devastating. Insouciance was the word that came to mind whenever I encountered Ethan. He carried himself with a teasing, devil-may-care manner. Pairing that with his tousled golden locks, flashing green eyes and body made for sin made him downright dangerous. Layer on his British accent, and it added up to way too much charm and temptation. He ruffled me in more ways than I liked to consider.

I'd only met him a few times and always in situations where the last thing on my mind should be anything to do with sex. Case in point—now. It was the middle of the night. I should be tired and cranky. Instead, I was on fire inside. All he had to do was look at me, and it was a direct shot of lust straight in my veins. To make matters worse, the last time I saw him, he kissed me. Inside of a few seconds, he'd left me hot and bothered. I hadn't forgotten that kiss, no matter how hard I tried. This annoyed me to no end. I didn't have time for men, much less an international sports star who was well known for being a relentless flirt. Hell, his nicknames in the press were *Golden Boy Brit* and *Magnum*.

My wandering eyes—naughty, willful eyes—took in his muscled shoulders and chest. Dear God, even his hands were sexy—strong and just battered enough you knew he could work magic with them. I heard a low chuckle from him and whipped my eyes up, feeling my cheeks heat. Dammit! I didn't need a sexy soccer star thinking I was ogling him.

"Should I repeat my question?" I asked, internally cringing at my bitchy tone. My default mode tended to be bitchy, especially when it came to men.

Ethan ran a hand through his rumpled hair, tossing a sheepish grin my way. The lower side of his jaw was slightly red. I presumed that was from the fist he allegedly walked into.

"No you shan't. I know it sounds ridiculous, but it's what happened. I was walking out and wasn't paying attention."

"So you walked into the guy's fist?"

Ethan threw another sheepish grin my way, a dimple appearing in one cheek. Sweet hell. He had a dimple I'd never even noticed. It only added to his roguish charm, which he already had in spades. My pulse was buzzing and heat slid through my veins. Even worse, I could feel the moisture at the apex of my thighs. This was a problem. I was contracted by the Seattle Stars on an as needed basis. My prior interactions with Ethan had been conveniently brief. With the exception of that out of the blue, knee buckling, body melting kiss. Well, that was brief too, yet so memorable it was seared into my brain and body. If he were actually charged with something over this silly bar fight, I'd have to spend much more time with him.

Potential epic disaster in the making as far as my sanity was concerned.

I opted to completely ignore my body's reaction to Ethan. Kind of hard to do seeing as my belly was doing somersaults, and I was getting so hot I needed a fan. But hey, I loved a challenge.

"So we're going with this whole stumbling into a fight then. I haven't had a chance to speak with the police. They sent me straight here when I arrived. When I do talk to them, will they tell me witnesses said otherwise?"

"Absolutely not," Ethan said, straightening in his chair. "I feel a bit foolish, but it's what happened."

His gaze was sober and earnest, his typical insouciance gone. I promptly discovered this was more dangerous than his teasing manner. A man as obscenely handsome and drool-worthy as him didn't need to be nice on top of it all.

What the fuck are you doing? Wipe the drool off your chin and do your damn job. If you do it well enough, you won't have to worry about seeing much of Ethan at all.

The next voice that tried to pipe up got kicked to the curb. That voice wanted to ask how come I was so damn determined not to even consider the possibility of a man in my life. Given how attractive Ethan was, it wouldn't be bad to enjoy some time between the sheets with him. I almost laughed hysterically. *Don't even go there.*

By sheer force of will, I met his eyes and nodded. I believed him, despite my inclination to give him a hard time. As I looked across the table, I found myself mesmerized by his eyes. They were a rich shade of green. Behind his teasing façade, I sensed there was more to the image he projected.

Didn't we just agree we weren't going there? You can't seriously be thinking Ethan would ever go for a woman like you. He's all about models and fun, not about a career-driven woman who works almost non-stop. Not to mention, the last thing he wants to deal with is an almost-thirty year old virgin.

He arched a brow, at which point I realized I was staring. I uncrossed my legs, immediately crossing them again. This had the unfortunate effect of drawing my attention to the fact the silk of my underwear was drenched. Great, just great. Ethan Walsh, a man I didn't want to want, had the ability to make me wet whilst sitting in a drab room at the Seattle Police Station.

This was annoying beyond belief. What had he just said? Oh right.

"Okay then. Well if that's the case, we should be able to clear this up right away."

I stood so quickly I knocked my chair over. Ethan was beside me in a flash. He caught the back of the chair in his hand and swung it back in place. Ever the teasing gentleman, he winked when he caught my eyes. He was too close. Even though I'd maybe been in close vicinity with him no more than three or four times, he was always a tad closer than I expected. He exuded strength and masculinity. My pulse bolted—if this was a race, my pulse was determined to win. I took a step back and bumped into the table.

Ethan's gaze held mine and then dipped down in a blatant perusal of my body. I should've been furious. If there was one thing I'd worked my tail off for, it was professional recognition. Instead, I was furious with myself for the subtle flush of enjoyment at knowing he noticed anything about me. The recollection of the feel of his lips on mine and his hard muscled body against me sent a hum through me. My skin prickled with heat under his attention—it was as if his gaze was caressing me. When his eyes meandered their way back to mine, my breath caught and my belly clenched, heat unfurling inside my core and radiating outward.

I forgot everything I'd been in the middle of. Hell, I forgot why I was there. Ethan stood just close enough, my brain simply fuzzed out, while my heart beat a wild, staccato rhythm. He lifted a hand, tracing a finger along my jaw and down the side of my neck. It was the hottest fucking thing anyone had ever done. I could feel the subtle roughness to the pad of that lone finger, all of my senses attuned to it. His touch was like a blaze of fire on my skin. I was hot all over and nearly melting inside.

I don't have any idea how much time passed, but his voice snapped me into awareness.

"Zoe luv..."

His pause dragged out just long enough, I feared he could hear the wild pounding of my heart. After a few beats where I could hardly breathe and desire rolled through me in a crashing wave, he finished his sentence.

"I shall have you one way or another."

Laced with his haughty British accent, his tone with a touch too confident for me. I was suddenly furious...and more turned on than I'd ever been in my entire life.

"Oh, I don't think so," I said, straightening my spine and glaring at him, doing my damnedest to ignore the thrumming need inside.

He grinned, a slow, devastating grin that made my insides do cartwheels and left me so hot and bothered I could barely think.

"We shall see about that," he said as he dropped his hand away.

I instantly missed the feel of that single point of contact. My eyes—damn eyes—had a mind of their own and flicked down, promptly noticing he was aroused. Very aroused. His cock was outlined against the faded denim that hugged his body like a lover. When I tore my eyes up and collided with his gaze, I saw the hint of devilry there and nearly ran from the room.

Chapter Three

ETHAN

"Please do explain," Coach said with a shake of his head as he eyed me.

I sat on the opposite side of his desk, while he idly tossed a ball back and forth in his hands. Coach Bernie Hoffman was a good guy. He also used to be the lion of football, excuse me soccer, back in his day before he retired and started coaching. In the year plus since I'd signed with the Stars, I'd come to respect the hell out of him. Unlike my last coach back in Britain, he had little tolerance for shenanigans. But he wasn't an ass about it. He never was. Hence, I felt foolish. Again.

"Coach, it's as I said. I know it sounds ridiculous, but I stumbled right into the middle of that fight. I'll fess up I was a bit sloshed, which is why I wasn't paying attention. But I swear, the other guy clocked me first. I can't believe he's pressing charges. Zoe suggested I could press charges in return, but that seems bloody ridiculous. Have you talked to her?"

The second I said Zoe's name, an image of her flashed in my mind—her cheeks flushed and her green eyes dark when

I teased her. I couldn't help myself. Bloody hell. That woman was so fucking hot, I almost got hard now thinking about her. Coach interrupted my lascivious train of thought.

"She emailed me sometime before the sun came up." He paused and shook his head again. "She didn't even hesitate when I asked her to go to the station and meet you at one in the morning. I hope you thanked her."

When he paused, I knew he expected me to say something. Affirmative, of course. As I mentioned, I had manners. "Absolutely. I thanked her several times."

Coach nodded slightly before continuing. "So yes, she sent an email giving me a status update. She doesn't seem concerned about your charges, and in fact, was pretty clear she thought you should push the issue with the police. She plans to go talk with them this morning when she can speak with a supervisor. My concern is this guy figured out who you were and might be thinking he can squeeze some money out of you."

I bit my tongue to keep from swearing. Running a hand through my hair, I sighed. "Are you serious? I didn't even think about that."

Coach nodded slowly with a roll of his eyes. "Wouldn't surprise me one bit. Anyway, Zoe will take care of it. If it's as you say, we shouldn't need to worry."

He stood and tossed the small ball into a basket in the corner. "Great work at practice today. Do me a favor and stay out of trouble, okay?"

I stood as he rounded his desk. "Of course. I won't even go to any pubs for now," I said, thinking it chafed to feel like some arse who'd been drunk and stupid.

I left his office and strolled down the hall to find my flat mate. I cornered the door into the locker room and almost collided with him.

"Eh, mate. Just coming to find you," I said as I turned to walk alongside him.

Tristan Wells glanced to me, flashing a slight grin. For

him, that was downright cheery. He was low-key, probably why he and I ended up such good mates. Tristan had signed with the Stars when I did, along with two other teammates from Britain. I'd known Liam and Alex back at university and ended up on a team in Britain with them after a stint with another that didn't go so well. We'd done the university bit together, so we knew each other well. Tristan was the brainiest of us all, hence why he hadn't been at university with us. Rather, he'd been at Oxford being brilliant. He also happened to be brilliant at football. At first, I'd considered him stuffy. He was bloody quiet. As I'd gotten to know him, I discovered he had a wicked, sly humor and wasn't the least bit stuffy.

He stayed quiet as we walked down the long stadium hallway, our footsteps echoing as we followed the curve of the hall to the doors. We stepped out into a rare, sunny afternoon for Seattle. Only then did Tristan speak.

"How'd it go with Coach?" he asked.

"Eh, fine," I replied with a shrug. "Said what I expected him to say. I shan't be having any nights out until this all goes away."

We commenced to walk to our flat. No surprise, but Tristan was quiet for a few moments. Every so often, I considered how surprising it might seem we'd become best mates. I'd be the first to admit, I was wild, flirty, teasing and generally out for fun however I could find it. Tristan, on the other hand, was somehow managing to balance a career in professional football whilst finishing his medical degree.

I loved women. Bloody hell did I love women. Tristan, on the other hand, seemed too damn busy to find time for them. He reminded me of Alex Gordon, another of our mates from Britain. Alex had approached sex like a business transaction back in London. An itch to be scratched and nothing more. Well, he'd gone and fallen like a rock for his girl Harper, but that was another thing.

Me? I loved sex, and I loved women. As much and as

often as I could find them. I hadn't given myself the nicknames stuck to me in the press, but I didn't mind them.
Magnum followed me from London, an ode to the condoms
a woman had quite publicly given to me after a night
together. Golden Boy Brit had been added to the list when I
moved here. That one amused me less so, nothing more than
a silly play off my hair. My sisters, all four of them, loved
teasing me with that one.

Tristan seemed mildly amused by all of this. He was the
best kind of mate. He never hesitated to pick up the phone,
including the other night when I needed someone sensible
to straighten out my unintended mess. As we came to a stop
at a cross street, he glanced my way. "Right then. You'd best
find another way to meet women. Else you'll drive me mad
moping about the flat," he said with a gleam in his hazel
eyes.

I elbowed him in the side as we started walking again. "I
don't need a pub to meet women."

He flashed another grin. "Aye, you don't. So who's the
poor lawyer that had to go meet you there last night?"

By the time I made it home last night, Tristan had been
asleep, understandably so. He'd been up and gone by the
time I woke up, so practice today was the first place we'd
spent more than a few minutes together.

"Same lawyer who handled Alex's case. Zoe Lawson."

Just saying her name made me jumpy. Bloody hell. I
wanted to see her again.

"Ah, the pretty redhead?"

The second Tristan asked his question, hot jealousy
coiled inside. Hot on its heels was me wondering what the
hell was going on. I didn't get jealous. Hell, I thought all men
should appreciate women. I'd even tried to set Tristan up
with a few women who were down for nothing but a little
fun. To no avail, of course. But still. I wasn't that guy who
growled about a girl and chased other guys off. I figured it
was easy come, easy go.

Apparently not with Zoe. Bloody hell.

I chided myself and told myself not to be crazy. Just because Tristan happened to notice Zoe was pretty didn't mean much of anything.

"Aye, the pretty redhead. Legs that go on for days," I finally managed, striving for casual.

We reached the steps to our building. Tristan glanced to me again, his gaze too sharp, too assessing. I ignored it as we walked into our flat. He tossed his keys on the table and kicked his shoes off. Our flat had an expansive living room and kitchen with sunlight spilling through the front windows and gleaming on the hardwood floors. To say our furnishings were minimalist might have been an understatement. We had a black sectional couch, a coffee table and a flat-screen television mounted on the back wall. The kitchen conveniently came with an island counter with stools for seating, so we didn't even have to bother with a table and chairs. Otherwise, we had our two bedrooms and a bathroom. We were both tidy. I loathed a messy place.

I kicked my shoes off and headed straight to the kitchen. I was bone tired from not much sleep and practice, so I started up some coffee. Tristan followed me over and slipped into a stool, running a hand through his black curls.

"I'd say you might have a thing for Zoe," he said. Out of the blue as far as I was concerned.

My pulse took off like a rocket, and I was relieved my back was to him. I bought myself a moment getting the water poured into the coffeemaker. Just enough time for me to talk my body down. It was bloody ridiculous the effect Zoe had on me. It occurred to me suddenly that last night, or this morning if that how you wanted to look at it, was the first time I'd actually been alone with her for more than a few minutes. My few and far between encounters with her before had always been in the company of Alex when he was dealing with his case last fall. Save when I'd impulsively kissed her in that hallway, which had been maybe a minute tops.

I tapped the button to start the coffee and turned to face Tristan, curling my hands over the counter as I did. It chafed at me to be bothered by his comment. Usually, I gave as good as I got, especially when it came to teasing about women. I'd managed to get my pulse to stop running about like a wild man, so I took that as a win. I met Tristan's gaze and knew in a flash he knew perfectly well I was bothered by Zoe. Fuck it. If I trusted anyone, it was Tristan.

"Perhaps I do," I said with a shrug, unable to resist the urge to sound as if it was nothing.

Tristan idly twirled a salt-shaker in his hand as he eyed me. I'd say he looked thoughtful, but he always looked thoughtful because he was one of the most sensible, thoughtful men I knew.

"Wouldn't be a bad thing to like a woman like her," he said. "That said, I don't think Zoe Lawson would fall for your fun and games. You'd have to take her seriously."

Oh, he had no idea how seriously I took Zoe. I'd felt many things in life, but uncertainty was not one of them. I ignored it because there was nothing else to do about a feeling like that. At least, not that I knew.

"Of course," I replied, bouncing my heel against the cabinet behind me. I took a breath and eyed Tristan, calling on the me I knew so well, the one who wasn't rattled by any woman. "Perhaps she needs to stop taking life so seriously?"

Tristan set the salt-shaker down and pushed off of his stool. "Perhaps. Or perhaps you might need a change of pace."

That left me speechless and unsettled. When I didn't reply, he started walking toward the bathroom. "I'm hitting the shower. My arm took a blow at practice today, and I could use more steam," he called over his shoulder.

I watched him walk away, annoyed with my irritation at him and at how unsettled I felt about his last comment. As soon as he disappeared from sight, I recalled Zoe's flushed cheeks and the feel of her silky skin under my fingertip. That one touch—a drag of my finger down her cheek and neck—and just thinking about it got me hard. Fuck it. I had good reason to go find her, so I would. I turned off the coffee and hollered to Tristan I was taking off.

Chapter Four

ZOE

"You can't be serious," I said.

"Zoe, I'm serious," Ted Duncan said. "Let me talk to my client and..."

"Ted, it's total bullshit and you know it. There are about thirty witnesses who said your client punched my client first," I countered, annoyed as hell to even be fielding this call.

Ted Duncan was the most obnoxious kind of attorney to be found. His face was plastered on billboards all over Seattle. He was litigation happy, promising his gullible clients dollar signs he rarely delivered. Now, he'd just informed me that his client, the drunk fool who'd been trying to fight with his friend and ended up punching Ethan instead, was considering suing Ethan over his bloody nose. Somehow between last night and this afternoon, the nose was now allegedly broken. I did *not* have time for this bullshit.

"Zoe, I will review the police reports, but my client's version of events is different, and he's concerned Mr. Walsh is receiving favorable treatment from the police, in addition to the alleged witnesses. Let's also not forget, this happened at a bar. It's fair to say every witness might have been under the influence," Ted said, his calm, measured and professional sounding tone at odds with everything he was doing.

I bit back my urge to swear and hang up on him. "Ted, I'll hear from you after you've had a chance to review the police reports from the event. If you weren't aware of this yet, the entire event was also captured on the security cameras at the bar."

"Oh? You don't say. Well, it's good to know we have concrete information," Ted replied. For the first time, I sensed a tiny bit of hesitation in him.

I smiled wryly to myself before politely saying goodbye and hanging up the phone. The second I did, it rang again. I glared at it and then realized it was Jana, my receptionist extraordinaire who also happened to be one of my best friends. I tapped the speaker button.

"Please tell me it's not Ted Duncan calling back." I might've enjoyed a moment of amusement when I sensed the dent in his smarmy armor, but I wasn't up for another chat with him just yet.

"It's not Ted Duncan calling back," Jana parroted cheerily.

I reached up and untied the knot in my hair, sighing at the feel of my hair falling loose. I was tired. I'd managed maybe two hours of sleep after rolling out of bed to meet Ethan at the police station. I could've seriously used a cup of coffee and then a long, hot bath.

"If it's not him, who is it?" I asked.

I heard footsteps, which let me know Jana was striding away from the reception desk. That meant she was stepping into the small room behind her desk, which she referred to as her top-secret gossip spot. It was the place she could go if she needed to convey something privately.

"Mr. Sexy is here to see you," she whispered into her headset.

My low belly clenched. "Mr. Sexy?"

"Don't play coy with me. Ethan Walsh is here. He's so hot, I could eat him up on the spot."

She paused. I knew she was grinning, and I knew she was waiting to see if I'd take her bait. I wasn't about to give her the satisfaction. I had no idea how, but she'd picked up I had maybe a thing for Ethan. Jana was crazy perceptive. Ethan had accompanied Alex to a meeting here at my office once. She'd quickly picked up on the fact I was a bit scatter-brained. I'd also made the mistake of telling her about that random kiss. She'd hardly shut up about it until I told her she was wasting her time. I knew I was in for it now that he would be around.

I was still toying with what to do about the fact we had kissed and he was now my client. Funny thing was, we lawyers had the loosest rules for ourselves. While plenty of us happily sued doctors who screwed their patients, we had this loosey-goosey rule on it. It was so loose that if your 'relationship' commenced before the client became your client, you were golden. Unless it wasn't consensual, but that was something else altogether. I found it wryly amusing that the fact Ethan had already kissed me might be the small detail that let me dance on the safer side of the ethics. That didn't change the fact it felt completely wrong and naughty. My intellect was slightly horrified at the fact my body only got more hot and bothered about it as a result.

"Well, he's yours to eat up," I countered, trying and utterly failing at tamping the tiny curl of jealousy. Jana wouldn't even think of making a play for a guy she thought I liked, but I desperately wanted to *not* want Ethan the way I did. My mind flashed to the blaze of fire his fingertip left behind on my skin last night. Or this morning, I supposed.

Just thinking about that tiny, brief touch, and I got hot all over.

"Oh hon, I can appreciate a sexy man, but I don't want to personally eat him up. I want you to," Jana said.

I could see the sly grin on her face. Of late, she'd been on me to ditch my virginity. She'd declared I was her project. I had mixed feelings about that. I was kind of annoyed I was still a virgin. It wasn't because I was a prude, or saving myself. No, it was as stupid as just being too focused on other things, namely my career. It didn't help I'd been a redheaded beanpole in high school and most of college. I'd been what people called a late bloomer. I didn't get curves until later. By that point, I was a tad bit self-conscious what with being teased for my height all the way up into my twenties.

"Hey Zoe, you there?" Jana asked.

"I'm here. Can you tell Ethan I'm busy?"

Jana sighed dramatically into my ear. "No, I'm not lying about your schedule. I'm telling him you'll be available in five minutes. Oh, and if you were hoping to throw me off the scent of how much you want to screw his brains out, trying to avoid him only proves my point."

"Jana, fuck off. Okay?"

Jana chuckled softly. "Don't you wish."

I could hear her footsteps and was about to hang up the line when I heard her speak again. She could've muted her speaker, but I knew she wanted me to hear her. Dammit. I wanted to hear Ethan.

"Mr. Walsh, do you mind waiting five minutes?"

"Be happy to," was Ethan's reply.

I could hear his teasing tone even in those three small words, and just the sound of it sent flutters twirling in my belly.

I was screwed. I had the hots for my client. Make that double screwed.

Restless, I stood up abruptly and dashed across my office to the decorative mirror between the windows. Oh hell. I'd temporarily forgotten I'd taken my hair down. It was a tousled mess now, and I didn't have time to fix it. I ran my fingers through it, trying to make it look tidy somehow. I almost always wore it up in a knot because my hair was wild. It was thick and wavy when it was loose. Nothing seemed to tame it, so I kept it out of the way. Throw in the fact it was a deep auburn and my hair drew way too much attention when it was loose. No one took me seriously then. All they did was stare at my hair. After getting teased so much about it when I was little, it was hard not to be self-conscious even though I intellectually knew it was silly.

There was a knock at my door, and I jumped away from the mirror. I couldn't believe I was obsessing about my appearance all because a client showed up unexpectedly. Well, not any client—the obscenely hot client whose kiss had left me hot, wet, and bothered and occupied nights of fantasies since.

Why not? Ethan's hot as hell. If you want to ditch your virginity, might as well make it worth your while.

My naughty voice was in full swing today. It was safe to say I hadn't heard much from this voice. Very few men caught my attention. If they did, they rarely noticed me, or not that I knew. Ethan had gone and set me loose inside with his random kiss months ago and then flirting so blatantly with me last night.

Another knock at my door. Right, I was dithering about how I looked while Ethan was waiting to meet with me.

I started to walk to the door when it opened and Jana slipped inside, closing it quickly behind her.

"What are you doing?" she asked, her voice just above a whisper.

My cheeks heated, and not for the first time, I silently cursed my fair skin.

"Nothing," I replied, striving to keep my voice calm and bored sounding.

Jana's perceptive gaze coasted over me. "Right. Nothing. Well, you look gorgeous. Good move to take your hair down," she said with a sly grin.

My cheeks got even hotter. "I did *not* take my hair down

for Ethan. I'm tired, and I took it down before. Trust me, I was just thinking about putting it back up, but..."

Jana shook her head. "Do *not* do that. I'd give an arm or a leg for your hair."

I rolled my eyes. "Whatever. Send Ethan in, would you? Let me get this over with," I replied, cringing a little at my snappish tone.

Jana eyed me for a moment and shook her head. "Just relax, okay? It's okay to think a guy's hot. You know I'm only teasing about him, right?"

"I know," I muttered. I took a gulp of air and straightened my shoulders. "And it's not okay to think one of my clients is hot, so this won't be going anywhere."

This was my first tacit admission that Jana was right. Her eyes took on a gleam.

"I think that makes it even more fun. What's more perfect than losing your virginity to a totally hot soccer star who happens to be your client?"

"It's not worth my career," I said flatly.

Jana put a hand on her hip. "Oh, get over yourself. You already kissed him when he wasn't your client, so you have some wiggle room." With a sly grin, she asked, "Ready for Mr. Sexy?"

I glared at her and walked back to my desk. I sat down quickly, needing the barrier to keep me sane when Ethan came in. I heard Jana speaking and then Ethan stepped through the door, and it was whisked shut behind him.

The second I looked up at him, my belly somersaulted, my pulse shot off like a rocket, and heat spread through my veins like wildfire. Sweet hell. He was too much. His golden hair was mussed, and his green eyes dark as he swept his gaze over me. He oozed raw masculinity and had the body to go with it. He wore nothing remarkable—just a navy t-shirt and jeans—yet somehow his clothes showcased his obscenely fit body. My mouth watered just looking at him—the corded muscles of his arms, his broad shoulders, and the way his jeans hung low on his hips, giving me a flash of bronzed skin and abs, just enough to make my panties wet.

Oh. My. God. I needed to get a grip.

Chapter Five

ETHAN

The door clicked shut behind me. I'd meant to say something flirty, just naughty enough to get under Zoe's skin and make her blush. But then I saw her. Her rich auburn hair was down, and the sight of it rendered me speechless. Seeing as I'd only seen her before when her hair was pulled back in a tidy knot, I had no fucking idea how wild her hair was. It fell in lush waves around her shoulders. Streaks of gold ran through the deep auburn, and the ends of her hair swirled just below her breasts. I knew what I wanted to see—her naked, riding me with that amazing hair letting me play peek-a-boo with her breasts.

Of course, I'd never seen her anything but fully clothed, every inch of her delectable body covered up. I had an excellent imagination however and could fill in the blanks perfectly well. Problem was, my cock twitched. Bloody hell. I couldn't be standing here with a hard-on in front of her—definitely not smooth. I forced my attention to her face. That didn't help. Her cheeks were flushed and her eyes bright. She stayed right where she was behind her desk.

Despite the blood rushing straight to my groin, I flashed her a grin. Old habits died hard after all.

"Hello, Zoe luv. How are you this afternoon?" I said as I strolled to take a seat in the chair across from her.

Her eyes flashed and her lips tightened. Perfect. Bloody perfect. I just needed to rattle her enough to get my footing. It was like sparring, and I loved it with her.

She drummed her fingertips on her desk and crossed and uncrossed her legs. I doubted that she ever considered the benefits of the modern desk she had. It had a sleek chocolate brown surface with nothing other than a slider for a keyboard. There was nothing to obstruct my view of her fantastic legs underneath. Really, it was a table with a keyboard tray and that's it. I fucking loved it. Even her legs were flushed. Okay, maybe best not to stare at her legs because now I had to talk my cock down again.

It suddenly occurred to me she hadn't even answered me yet. "Did you forget how to say hello?" I asked.

I'd be the first to admit, half the reason I got my reputation as a player and a flirt was because when I wasn't sure what to do, teasing was my fallback position.

Zoe's cheeks flushed deeper. She uncrossed and crossed her legs again.

"Shall we go for a walk?"

"Excuse me?" she countered, her voice a tad snippy.

Oh this was perfect. I loved riling her up. She didn't let much through, but her cheeks were pink and her eyes pinned me with a haughty glare.

"Well, you seem a little restless. I thought perhaps a walk might help," I said in my most polite, bland tone.

Zoe's lips parted, which drew my attention to her perfect mouth. Bloody hell. Her lips were plump, soft and pink. I was torn between remembering what it felt like to kiss her and what it would feel like to see those perfect lips wrapped around my cock. Oops. Not a good idea to let myself think like that. Way too distracting.

Zoe uncrossed her legs again, and I could've sworn I saw a glimpse of black silk between her thighs. Wow. If she had any idea of the view I had, I was certain she'd be replacing her desk post haste. I could only imagine how many men had sat here and enjoyed the view of her legs and trying to catch a glimpse of her panties. She was wearing another fitted skirt. She seemed to like those. I glanced up to find her still glaring at me.

"We don't need to take a walk. Perhaps you could let me know your reasons for stopping by," she said, all prim and proper.

"Coach mentioned you were planning to follow up with the police again today, so I thought I'd stop by and chat about that."

She spun in her chair to face the computer screen at an angle on her desk. "Of course, let me check to see if the lead officer has replied to my email yet."

I waited quietly, watching her as she clicked and scrolled through something on the computer screen. After a moment, she spun back to face me. Definitely black silk. My eyes had a mind of their own, and I couldn't help but peek again.

"Okay, here's where we stand. We're going to let them try to talk some sense into the guy charging you. The problem they have is if they don't charge you while there were witnesses who saw you hit him, it looks bad. They're recommending you support them filing charges against him."

"But that's bloody ridiculous! I don't think the fool meant to hit me. He meant to sock his mate. I just got in the way. Why can't he leave well enough alone like me?"

Zoe was all business now and back in her element. She exuded a sharp confidence. "Because people are foolish and stupid sometimes."

"Coach is worried this guy thinks he's got leverage and I've got money he can chase."

Zoe shrugged. "Maybe so, but I don't think we need to

worry about that. If he wants to make it a nuisance for you, he can. I'll handle it. The entire incident is on the security cameras, so I think you'll be fine no matter what."

I nodded, pondering that the last fucking thing I wanted to deal with was some bullshit legal issue, but whatever. I loved my job. I mean, for crying out loud, I balled for money. I'd take my lumps when I had to. It was just bloody stupid that I walked into the guy's fist. Had I not been sloshed, I'd have been less likely to reflexively swing at him. But it was what it was. I had complete confidence in Zoe. I also wanted to get in her black silk panties.

I ordered myself to behave. At least for a few more minutes. "Right then. If you say so, I believe you."

There was a knock at her office door. Zoe stood and walked to open it. I turned in my chair, eating up the sight of her body. Her skirt fell to just above her knees. It was proper enough, but she had a lush bottom, which filled it out perfectly. Her glorious hair swung with her steps. Fuck me. I wanted to wrap it around my hand and kiss her senseless.

She opened the door, and I heard her friendly receptionist say something. They kept their voices low so I couldn't hear what she was saying. I didn't realize I was standing and walking toward her as she closed the door until I was almost there. Bloody hell. This woman was like my own personal magnet. My body just did its thing. I was accustomed to being more calculated when it came to women. I couldn't have calculated what happened next, but it was fucking perfect.

Zoe turned back. She was in her all-business mode and moving fast. She never even looked up, and she was walking so fast, I didn't have a chance to react. In two strides, she collided with me.

"Oh! I..."

Her breath came out in a whoosh, and her eyes widened. She was right up against me, and my body had something to say about that. Hell, my cock had been at half-mast ever since I laid eyes on her today. The feel of her full breasts against me, the heat of her body and the flush on her cheeks —all inside of a second and I was rock hard. I knew she could feel it against her because it was impossible to miss.

I didn't really care to play it smooth just now. It felt too good to have her this close. I was surprised she didn't jump back, but she didn't. I lifted a hand and ran it through the ends of her hair. Her hair alone was an unholy temptation. It was soft and silky. The back of my fingers brushed across her blouse, and I could feel her nipple pebbling through the thin cotton.

Lust scored me straight through. I wanted Zoe. I wanted her like mad. I looked to her. Her cheeks were flushed, and there were tiny freckles scattered across the bridge of her nose and her cheeks. I'd never given a thought to freckles. Hell, I'd never even noticed them on anyone. On her, they were another thing I was suddenly enamored with. I wanted to peel off her clothes and find every freckle on her body, preferably with my lips.

I could feel her breath coming in shallow pants. Her pulse fluttered in her neck. Well, I'd been waiting to kiss her again. Now seemed like the perfect time.

"Zoe."

Her eyes whipped up, a swirl of green and gold growing darker by the second.

"Yes?" she asked in a breathy whisper.

Oh that did it. I'd meant to say something witty, to tease her a bit. But all I wanted was to kiss her.

I slid my hand up under her hair and cupped her nape, prepared for her to shove me away at any second. She didn't. I waited a beat. I suppose I was a glutton for punishment because I fully expected her to knee me in the balls at any second. I loved how tall she was. She fit against me just so. I barely had to tilt my head to kiss her. I meant to go slow. What I meant to do and what I did when it came to Zoe were never the same thing, or so it was coming to seem.

The moment I brought my lips to hers, she tensed. I thanked every god I could think of when she didn't shove me away.

"Ethan?"

Somehow she managed to say my name against my lips. This, of course, got me even harder.

"Yes?" I countered, not moving an inch.

"Mm...what...?" She paused and moved back incrementally.

Well, now this would not do.

Her eyes locked to mine, searching. Something flashed in the depths of hers, but it came and went so fast I couldn't interpret it.

"What are you doing?"

Her voice was all husky and breathy and made me want to spin her around, bend her over the desk and shove her skirt up.

Pump the brakes, mate. Zoe is not that kind of girl.

I wanted her so much, I could barely think. I stared into the layers of her eyes—green dusted with gold and flecked with brown. With her wild hair tumbling about her shoulders, her pink cheeks and her plump lips, it was a fucking miracle I kept a leash on myself.

"Kissing you," I belatedly replied.

I kept expecting her to shove me away, but she didn't. She shifted on her feet, her eyes scanning my face. She bit her lip, her teeth denting the delectable cushion.

"I don't think that's a good idea," she finally said.

Mind you, she said that, but she didn't fucking move an inch and every curve of her front was pressed against me with my cock nestled in the cradle of her hips.

"And why not?" I countered.

"Because you're my client, and..."

"Unless I think it's a problem, how is it a problem?" I asked, injecting a touch of haughty in my tone.

Her eyes narrowed. Fuck it. I wasn't waiting to debate

this with her. I dipped my head and fit my mouth over hers. Little did I know she'd be opening her mouth to say something. Perfect. I swept my tongue inside, tangled my hand in her hair and devoured her mouth. If she really thought kissing me was a problem, she seemed to immediately forget that. Her tongue warred with mine.

When I slid my hand down her spine and cupped her bottom, pulling her tight against me, she moaned in my mouth. That did it. Holding her tight to me, I took a few steps until her back bumped against the door. My palm flat against it, I drew back, catching her bottom lip in my teeth before drawing my tongue along the soft skin of her neck. She tasted so fucking good—a little sweet, a little tangy. I needed more. I tore at her blouse to find proper Zoe had a thing for naughty lingerie. Her full breasts were encased in sheer black silk, her pink nipples taut and begging for me to taste them. So I did. I laved my tongue over the silk, grinning when she moaned.

Chapter Six

ZOE

Ethan's mouth closed over my nipple, and I almost melted to the floor. Sweet hell. Just kissing him sent me tumbling into madness, yet this was beyond good. The hot, wet suction of his mouth and the nip of his teeth while he rolled my other nipple between his fingers nearly made me come on the spot. Hot shivers raced over my skin while my pulse skittered wildly. I could hardly breathe with my breath coming in pants and gasps.

I should've been mortified. My God. I was making out in my office with one of my clients. And not just any client, but a high profile sports star. If anyone found out about this, it could seriously dent the entirely respectable reputation I'd cultivated.

Attorneys weren't supposed to fuck their clients.

Problem was, thinking about how I wasn't supposed to be doing this only made me hotter. I could feel the wet silk between my thighs and shifted my legs, anything to relieve the need there.

Ethan drew back, catching my nipple lightly in his teeth as he did and sending a hot jolt of pleasure to my core. He lifted his head, his hooded green gaze locking with mine. I expected him to tease but he didn't. He just looked at me, the air heavy around us.

My heart thudded against my ribs. The longer his gaze held mine, the hotter I got inside. I was so wet, I could feel the moisture on the insides of my thighs. His cock was hot and hard against me, the feel of it making me want him inside of me. I wished for the thousandth time I wasn't still stuck a virgin. If Ethan knew, he'd likely bolt out of my office so fast, he'd leave skid marks behind him.

He pinched my nipple, and a little moan escaped. I was so flushed all over, I doubted he could notice I got even more flushed at that. His mouth curled at one corner in a devilish grin. I should've gotten annoyed with that. Instead, my body, traitor that it was, only tightened further in anticipation.

One last tease of my nipple and his hand slid down over my belly. It just now occurred to me he'd unbuttoned my blouse and my skirt was riding up my thighs. His hand kept going, curling over the curve of my hip and down along my thigh. My legs were bare, and the feel of his calloused palm against my skin made me so crazy I shifted my legs again. Oh. My. God. I was so far gone I almost came just from moving my legs.

"Before I go, I need to know one thing," he said, his voice low and taut.

I was so bad off, everything he did made me want him even more. My belly clenched at the sound of his voice.

"What's that?" I asked, my voice raspy and need galloping through me so hard and fast I could barely breathe.

He shoved my skirt up and trailed his fingers up along the inside of my thigh. "I want to know if you're as wet as I'm hard."

I swallowed, flushing all over again. I couldn't have stopped him if I tried and I didn't want to. He lightly stroked a finger over the silk of my panties, never once looking away from me. His half-grin disappeared and his eyes went dark.

He dragged his finger over the silk again before pushing back abruptly. At that moment, there was a sharp knock on my door. No one but Jana knocked on my door, but the last thing I needed was her to open it and find me like this—my shirt unbuttoned, my bra damp, my nipples so tight they ached, and my skirt up to my waist.

Flustered, I kept my back flat against the door. Ethan shifted back to a teasing grin, his eyes flicking from me to the doorknob.

"I'll be out in a few minutes, Jana," I called, striving to keep my tone normal.

"Okay, your four o'clock appointment is here," she said, her voice muffled through the door.

At the sound of her footsteps retreating, I glared at Ethan. "This is *not* funny."

I pushed away from the door and yanked my skirt down. Before I had a chance to button my shirt, he was immediately in front of me again. Without a word, he buttoned my blouse, pausing between my breasts, his eyes flicking up to mine.

"I didn't figure you for a black silk girl," he said with another half-grin.

Dear God. He was going to make me lose my fucking mind. All he had to do was throw one of those devastating grins my way and I almost melted to the floor.

I couldn't even formulate a reply with my heart banging wildly, my belly somersaulting and my channel throbbing with need. He pinched one of my nipples before buttoning the rest of my blouse.

He held still, and I could feel his hard shaft nestled against me again. I didn't want him to leave. That's how far gone I was. I had another client waiting to see me, and if Ethan had pushed even the slightest bit, nothing would've kept me from finally saying goodbye to my virginity. Right here in my office.

He reached up and brushed my hair back away from my face. "You shouldn't wear your hair down when you're working," he said gruffly.

"Huh?" was my brilliant reply.

"You're too fucking beautiful as it is, but with your hair down, you're downright dangerous. No man can see you and not want you," he said bluntly. "I said I'd have you, and I will, but I don't intend to share."

His gaze had gone somber, while all I could do was gape at him. I was so caught in the wild beat of my desire for him, I could barely think. He was worried about my hair?

"Share?" I asked dumbly.

He shrugged, that insouciance he wore so well coming the fore. "Right. I don't want your four o'clock appointment coming in and getting off on looking at you."

I had no idea what to say. My mouth opened and closed. Finally, I gave my head a shake and tried to focus. A bit difficult with his cock hot and hard and nestled against my core. Hell, all of him was hard. His body was like an in-the-flesh example of the perfect male specimen—all honed muscle and sinew. Another shake of my head, and I managed to form words.

"Ethan, men don't notice my hair. They don't notice me. Trust me on this."

He arched a brow. "Yes they do, luv. You don't pay attention. You're too busy being proper. Trust me on this."

A laugh escaped as I stared at him. He stepped back and reached up, sliding his hands through my hair. After a second, I realized he was actually trying to put my hair up.

This time I really laughed and swatted at his hands. "Oh stop. I'll do it. I usually leave it up, but I didn't know you were coming in, and I hardly got any sleep last night," I said as I quickly spun my hair into a knot.

I walked to the mirror and smoothed it back from my

forehead. Wild though my hair could be, it was long enough to easily tie into a knot. I strode to my desk and snagged two bobby pins from the paperclip holder before returning to the mirror to pin the knot in place.

I wasn't really thinking. It was all too much and too crazy what I'd just allowed to happen with Ethan. My body was thrumming with need. I spun back to find him standing by my desk, his eyes watching me.

"Have dinner with me," he said abruptly.

One look in his eyes, and I nearly melted right where I was. But I couldn't. This was insane. I couldn't date a client. Not to mention if Ethan knew I was a virgin, he wouldn't even consider me. He was a player, and I knew it. Good God, the man was in the gossip news all the time, mostly known for his healthy appetite for women and for being plain handsome as all hell.

I started to shake my head, and he shook his right back at me. "Don't tell me no. I know you want me."

Even though his words sounded cocky, his tone sounded earnest.

"Ethan, it's not that, and it's not just because you're my client. That's a thing, but I'm not exactly the kind of girl you go for."

His eyes narrowed, and he arched a brow. "I think it's pretty obvious you are," he said, his tone droll.

Next thing I knew, I went and said the stupidest thing ever. "I seriously don't think you're into virgins."

The second the words flew out of my mouth, I wanted to die. Right there. My face got hot. I fought the urge to run right out of my office because that only meant running right into Jana and my next client.

Ethan's eyes widened. He opened his mouth and then snapped it shut. He stared at me, hard, for a few beats and then straightened, walking to stand just in front of me.

"Oh no, luv. That's not a problem."

Chapter Seven

ETHAN

I hung back on the pitch and watched the play. Liam, as usual, had set our offense up beautifully. He'd just nicked one in the goal and was already bringing the ball back up the field. I wasn't sure what was up with the opposing team tonight because the last time we played them, they worked our defense to exhaustion. Tonight, I had to be on my game, but it was a light game for the defense. Not much later, I walked off the pitch with Alex Gordon at my side. Alex was one of the best goalkeepers in professional play anywhere in the world. If you asked me, that is. Nice thing was, pretty much anyone who knew anything about pro football, excuse me soccer here in the US, agreed.

I glanced to him. Alex was forever serious. He'd just locked the opposing team out completely and didn't even seem to notice. He dragged his sleeve across his face and glanced to me, his brown eyes catching mine. "Good game, eh?"

"It was a bloody easy win."

He grinned, just barely. "That it was." He started to say something else as we entered the stadium hallway leading toward the locker room, but he came to a stop, a slow grin spreading across his face. That grin meant only one thing. His girl Harper was here. I glanced ahead to see her weaving through the players ahead of us. She reached Alex, and he swung her up against him, drawing her close for a kiss.

Serious Alex wasn't so serious when it came to Harper Jacobs. He'd fallen for her like a rock sinks to the bottom of the ocean. Thank fucking god she kept his head above water after that. She wiggled her way down and glanced to me.

"Hey Ethan, another win," she said with a smile. "You guys barely broke a sweat."

"Well, your boy here made it bloody hard for the other guys to score. Made my job even easier."

Harper looped her arm around Alex's waist as he pulled her to his side and kept on walking to the locker room. With her glossy brown hair and bright blue eyes, Harper was lovely. I could objectively notice that but didn't feel the slightest pull for her. We chatted casually as we walked to the locker room. Alex dipped his head for a kiss before stepping away from Harper. I never paid much attention to my mates and their loves, but I couldn't help but notice Alex and Harper now. Their mutual desire was plainly obvious, as was the tenderness in Alex's eyes. He was crazy protective of her, but Harper was a strong woman and held her own.

I gave my head a shake. What the fuck was I doing staring at them? It wasn't like I gave a damn about their constant PDA, but all I could think was what it might be like to have something like that with Zoe. Another hard shake of my head, and I made my way into the locker room. A scalding hot shower might get my mind off of Zoe. Problem was ever since she'd dropped her little bomb the other day, I could hardly stop thinking about her.

The noise of the locker room faded when I stepped into the showers, heading to the far corner. With water sluicing over me, all I could think about was the way it felt to kiss her.

Some kind of mad, insane heaven. She was so fucking hot and she had no clue. Her mouth was an unholy temptation. And her body? Fuck me. It took all I had not to rip her clothes off and fuck her right there, and that was before I knew she was a virgin. I recalled her taut nipples under the black silk.

Mate, you can't be fantasizing about Zoe here unless you want a cock stand for everyone to see.

I forced my thoughts off of her nipples, but my mind went straight to the feel of her against me. She was tall with those legs that went on forever. Her skin was like silk. Her panties had been drenched. I'd meant to tease her, but I hadn't anticipated what it would do to me. I'd barely held onto my control. That wasn't a problem I ever had. I loved to drag things out, to tease a girl until she was wild. Once again, what I meant to do and what happened with Zoe never turned out to be the same thing.

Hell, I'd gone into her office fully intending to find a chance to kiss her. I'd thought I'd tease her, have a little fun and leave her hot and bothered. I bloody nailed leaving her hot and bothered. Problem was, I left her office so hard I had to go back to my flat and take matters into my own hands. Literally. I was bloody certain that hadn't happened since my grammar school days. There were many perks to being a pro-footballer. Back in London, you were practically royalty. Hell, just about anywhere in the world. America was a bit behind the times with the hero worship of soccer players, as they dubbed us, but we had our pick of women anywhere we went. I hadn't had to trouble myself to find a girl since I left for university.

Under usual circumstances, if I had a raging hard on, I found myself a more than willing woman. At the moment, no woman other than Zoe appealed to me. Just thinking about scouting about for one nearly bored me to tears. Coach's warning that I needed to steer clear of pubs would be no trouble. Problem was, how the hell did I persuade Zoe to stop being so uptight about this whole client thing? And was I insane enough to chase after a virgin?

I pondered that question as I toweled off and tossed my clothes on. Out of habit, Tristan and I walked to our flat together. Some nights, I might leave him behind to go out looking for fun. Tonight, I appreciated his typical quiet. I was pondering how the hell it could be Zoe was a virgin. I mean, I knew with utter certainty that she hadn't gone through life without turning heads. She was bloody gorgeous. Oh, she gave off that buttoned up, proper air for certain. I grinned thinking about how tidy she looked when I left. Her blouse was perfectly in place and her skirt pulled back to its demur length. My mind flashed to the way she'd looked before with her breasts nearly spilling out of her black silk bra, her nipples perked up, and her skirt up around her waist.

Bloody hell. I couldn't be walking around with a cock stand all the time.

Within a few minutes, I followed Tristan into our flat, heading straight for the refrigerator. A glance inside reminded me it was my turn to do the grocery run this week.

"Aw hell. I forgot to take care of the groceries," I said, straightening and letting the refrigerator door fall closed.

Tristan flashed a grin and shrugged. "No worries, mate."

"Oh no. It's a worry. I'm bloody starving. Pizza?"

At Tristan's nod, I slipped my phone out of my pocket and promptly dialed our preferred delivery place.

A bit later, we were lounging on the sofa with the pizza on the coffee table. I finished off a slice and eyed Tristan. I had a question and one I wouldn't ask many of my mates. In fact, likely only Tristan because I trusted him completely. Problem was, I couldn't believe what I was pondering.

I'd never actually had sex with a virgin. I knew some guys thought it was a thing, but it had never been something I chased after. Zoe dropping that little bomb would normally have sent me the other direction. Instead, the opposite seemed to be happening. All I could think about was her. Even worse, I was worried about it. To be honest, I was a player and I damn well knew it. I liked to have fun and keep things light and easy. I made sure I left women satisfied and figured all was in good fun. But...a virgin? I was having nightmares it would be horrible somehow. I had four sisters I could ask, but I wasn't about to do that. We were close, but there was no way I wanted to know about their respective first experiences, nor to hear what they might have to say about me even asking them something along these lines.

Tristan had his own sisters and I figured him to be one of the more sensitive mates I knew. Right then. I'd simply ask him.

What I meant to be a question came out not quite so. "Zoe's a virgin."

"What the hell, mate? Are you announcing random facts about women now?" Tristan asked as he sputtered on a swallow of his beer.

The funny moment steadied me. I handed him a napkin from the coffee table. After he wiped his chin, he eyed me for a long moment, his way too perceptive gaze boring into me.

"You're telling me this, why?" he finally asked.

I grabbed another slice of pizza and took a bite. I needed something to do to keep from squirming where I sat. After another few bites, I'd basically inhaled the poor pizza slice. I eyed Tristan and shrugged. "Uh, dunno why I'm telling you," I finally said.

He gulped down some water and looked back my way. "Right. You don't know. Perhaps it's because you've got it bad for her and haven't a bloody clue what to do about it?"

I almost choked on the bite of pizza I'd just taken. I should've known better than to try to ask Tristan anything. He was too damn perceptive. There was that and the fact he wasn't a player, not like me. Rather, he approached women as an interruption to the deeper pursuits of his brain.

Beyond playing ball, his only passion was medicine. At least, as far as I could tell. He didn't avoid women. In fact, the few I'd known him to be involved with were absolutely gaga for him. Back in London, he had a long-term dalliance with a girl he'd gone to university with. It was strictly business. She was as cool and guarded as he was. They had sex, they kept it casual, and there were definitely no messy emotions to inter-fere with his life.

You asked him for a bloody good reason, and he's right. You've got it bad for Zoe and you have no idea what to do.

All of this would be so much simpler if she weren't a virgin. I wished like hell I didn't know that giant detail.

"Don't see why it should be a thing. If you like her, do something about it. Though I'd wager she's not the kind of woman you usually chase after. Like I said before," Tristan said, interrupting my train of thought.

Annoyance flashed through me. "Now why do you say that?"

I didn't share that Alex had said something to the same effect once before. I might like to have a little fun, but I wasn't an asshole. Nor was I an idiot.

"Because she's the real deal man. She's obviously a damn good attorney, brilliant if her reputation means anything. She's gorgeous too. However, she's not the kind of woman to be charmed by a pro athlete. You won't be finding her at the pubs or anything like that. Never know though. Maybe she wants the same kind of casual thing you prefer. Work seems to be her priority," Tristan replied.

I stared at him. The side of me I knew so well—the easy-going player side—thought perhaps that would be ideal. I'd show Zoe what she'd been missing all these years and then move along. Strange thing was, this other side of me—one with whom I wasn't too familiar—didn't like that so much. Zoe deserved more than a roll in the sheets. Bloody hell. I'd made a muck of things, and I hadn't even gotten started yet.

My silence must've lasted a bit too long. Tristan shook

his head slowly. "Mate, I know you've got it bad when you haven't got a thing to say. I'm betting you meant to ask my advice. Not that it's worth much, but you'll get it. Zoe's top shelf. Treat her like she should be treated. The virgin part, I wouldn't worry so much about. Unless you meet her at her level, it won't matter."

I was entirely unaccustomed to anyone implying I couldn't get a woman I wanted and was affronted. It didn't help that I was feeling uncertain, something I couldn't ever recall feeling when it came to women. As such, all I could manage was a muttered curse at Tristan. "Fuck off. If I want Zoe, I'll have her."

He grinned. "Aye then. Let me know how it goes."

Chapter Eight

ZOE

"Oh my God, you're being ridiculous," Jana said with a shake of her head.

I rolled my eyes. "I'm not. Ethan is way out of my league."

Jana finished chewing the bite of omelet she'd just taken and brushed her hair off her shoulder—her hair was naturally brown with streaks of purple and burgundy. With her typically eye catching hair colors, wide blue eyes, porcelain skin and hourglass figure, she tended to draw attention no matter where we were. At the moment, we were having breakfast at a nondescript diner before heading into the office. The man seated at the booth across from us had spent the last half hour eyeing Jana while she was entirely oblivious. The diner in question was aptly named West Coast Diner. The simple name was befitting its simple location in a square building with silver flashing and a neon sign. It wasn't fancy, but the food was sublime. We met here once or twice a week before going into the office.

Jana set her fork down and rested her elbows on the table, her eyes narrowing as she considered me. "Trust me,

Ethan Walsh has the hots for you. He could barely stop staring at you when I came in because you were making your next appointment wait too long, and I couldn't miss the fact you two looked like you'd been making out," she said with a sly grin.

My cheeks flamed. I bought some time by taking a gulp of coffee and waving for our waitress to get me a refill. I'd been beyond flustered by the time Ethan left my office the other day. That had been a full four days ago, and not an hour had passed since that I wasn't replaying those heated moments. Just now, my mind flashed to the teasing feel of his fingers dragging across the wet silk of my panties. Oh hell. Just thinking about it elicited a throb of need between my thighs. I'd managed to avoid Jana's prying questions at the time because I had an impatient client waiting. I let that appointment run late because I knew she had to leave for her exercise class. She'd been gone when I finally emerged from my office.

I'd been waiting for her to say something for days and had almost, not quite but almost, convinced myself she must not have noticed that my clothes had been hastily put back in place and my hair wasn't as tidy as usual. I should've known she was letting me fret and waiting to pounce.

I sighed and glared at her. "I don't know what you mean," I finally hedged.

Jana threw a glare right back at me. "Hon, I've had way more experience with men than you. I know how I look after I make out with someone in the office."

"You make out with guys at the office? When do you have time for that?"

That earned me a slow eye roll. "Not since I've been working for you, but you do remember why I left my last job, right?"

"Oh right. I forgot."

Jana had a hot and heavy relationship with her last boss who'd lied to her about the tiny detail of his marriage. When she discovered the truth, she promptly quit, but not before her reputation took a hit. She'd been a paralegal at a major law firm in Seattle. She should've been an attorney, but she only made it halfway through law school when her younger sister was diagnosed with breast cancer and died. Between that and the sordid details that leaked out about her alleged affair, well, to say her career had been derailed was an understatement. She'd been a friend in law school, so I'd reached out and offered her a job. We'd gone from being sort of friends to the best of friends since then.

I finally looked over at her and sighed. "Right. Okay. Maybe he kissed me." The second I said it, I wanted to take it back. Jana was on a stupid mission to get me to say goodbye to my virginity. I kept telling her I was too busy.

On its face, that was true. I worked all the time. I'd known from the start of my legal career that I didn't want to try to do the big firm thing. Women had it twice as hard as men, if not more so, trying to climb the ladders of prestige and recognition. I'd done as I set out to do and started my own legal practice, which meant if I wanted decent pay and clients I had to work my ass off to make it happen. It wasn't hard for me to keep focused on work. I mostly focused on defense cases, but I did a bit of everything. I'd had a few lucky breaks with high profile clients who recommended me to others. The impatient client who met with me after I made out with Ethan in my office was the no-nonsense father of a son who got good and drunk one night and got lucky enough to get stopped by a police officer before he made it out of the parking lot at a bar. His son was friendly and typically short on judgment for a barely legal college kid. Anyway, he gave my name to the Seattle Stars when they were scouting for an attorney for a player a year ago. Since then, the team called on me whenever they had a player who needed help.

Circling back to Jana's mission—well, I didn't know when I'd find time to have sex. Ethan had rebounded quickly and

was so ridiculously suave he managed to tease me, but I'd
seen the shock in his eyes when I blurted out I was a virgin.
At twenty-nine, I knew I was bordering on ancient to
somehow have managed this accidental feat. In my defense,
I did date in college. I wasn't a prude, and I certainly wasn't
saving myself. But when I'd found time to date, most of the
guys just didn't do it for me. I'd made it to all the bases but
home. I sighed internally. At my age, the situation was a
nuisance.

It annoyed the hell out of me that part of me hoped my
thoughtless announcement of my virgin state to Ethan
would chase him off, while another part of me was let down
that would probably be the case. Ugh.

Jana cleared her throat. I hadn't noticed I was staring at
the table while I obsessed over how ridiculous I was being. I
looked back up to her to find her piercing blue eyes on me.

"Oh hon, Ethan is the kind of guy that ties most women
in knots. No need to beat yourself up over that. He's the
perfect candidate for your little project," she said with a hint
of a grin.

"It's not my project," I grumbled. "It's yours and it's
stupid."

Our waitress hurried past and filled our coffees before
whirling away. Jana took a sip of hers and leaned back. "Okay
fine. I'll agree it's not exactly your thing. But I'm only on a
mission because you're headed toward serious spinsterhood
if you don't get over it and lose your virginity. It's turning
into a *thing*. You're gorgeous and brilliant, and you need to
relax and have some fun. Hell, at least half of the women in
Seattle are panting after Ethan, and he likes you. Have fun
and then you can stop worrying about your virginity being an
issue."

"Geez, Jana. You make it sound like I worry about this. I
don't..."

She cut right in. "Oh sure, you don't think about sex

much, but that's because you keep saying this gets in the way."

I glared at her and wished maybe I hadn't been so honest about everything. I leaned my chin in my hand and sighed. "Fine. Yes, it gets in the way, but I don't really have time to date." Aside from my career focused life getting in the way, I'd heard from enough men I was too intimidating. I knew it didn't help to be as tall as most men and not give a damn about stroking their egos. In the world of attorneys, plenty of men went around with their chests puffed out. I enjoyed beating them at their own game, which seemed to have given me a rep as a ball-buster.

"Well, it doesn't sound like you need time if you were making out in the office with Ethan," Jana said with a wink.

"I can't believe you're supporting office sex," I muttered.

"Hey, it was fun until I discovered he was married. Don't knock office sex, hon. It's totally hot."

I was saved from further mortification when our waitress raced by and our check fluttered out of her hand onto the table. Jana's phone conveniently jingled at the same time.

"Have to take this, it's my mom," she said quickly before answering.

I took care of the check, and we walked to the office a few blocks away. Jana chatted on the phone with her mom, while I wondered when I might see Ethan again and utterly failed at shushing my naughty thoughts.

Chapter Nine

ETHAN

I jogged up the stairs in Zoe's office building. She'd left Coach a message about an update. I was peeved she hadn't called me directly, but I could guess why. It had been a full week since I'd last seen her and kissed her senseless. Or maybe she kissed me senseless. I didn't give a damn. I'd gotten my head screwed on straight and wasn't wobbling over her anymore. I figured it was perfect. She'd never had sex, so it'd be ideal for me to take care of that for her. Tristan was probably right. Work was her thing, so I didn't need to worry she'd read too much into anything with me.

With my groove firmly back, I blew through the door into the reception area of her office to find her receptionist finishing a call. Under usual circumstances, I'd think her receptionist was hot. She had dark hair streaked with bright colors and a body of juicy curves. Odd thing was, I could only appreciate her in the abstract. A tiny worry nudged me in the back of my mind. It was rare for me not to settle in and appreciate the hell out of a woman like her. The fact I didn't reminded me I hadn't looked at any woman that way since Zoe had shown up in the middle of the night to help me out with my annoying legal problem.

I kicked that worry to the curb and waited while the receptionist finished her call. All I could think about was when I could get myself behind the door to Zoe's office and kiss her again. When she did, she looked up at me with a wide smile, her blue eyes bright against her fair skin. She seemed amused by something, but I was too focused on seeing Zoe to wonder what.

"Hello, Mr. Walsh. I don't think you're on Zoe's schedule. Would you like me to see if she's available?" she asked.

That told me Zoe *was* available, otherwise she'd be letting me know Zoe was with a client. "I'd like that. Thank you."

She tapped something in her keyboard and then glanced to me again. "I don't think I had a chance to introduce myself. I'm Jana. I'm Zoe's receptionist and paralegal. If she's not available, you can let me know if there's anything I can help with."

"Oh no. I'll wait as long as I need to."

Because I bloody would. I wasn't leaving without seeing Zoe.

Jana arched a brow and a subtle gleam entered her eyes. "Okay then."

Her eyes flicked from me to her computer screen. She stood quickly and held a finger up. "Just a minute."

She stepped from behind the curved desk and around the corner where the door to Zoe's office was. As soon as I heard the door open and close, I leaned over the desk and looked at her computer screen. My guess was she'd messaged Zoe, and I figured Zoe was stalling. The exchange I read in the screen Jana had conveniently left open promptly put her on my list of favorite people.

Jana: Mr. Sexy is here to see you!

Zoe: I'm busy.

Jana: No you're not. You have no appointments for two hours.

I'm working on the draft order for the SA case. Nothing else is a rush. Get that man in your office and do him. Now!

Zoe: OMG. I'm not 'doing' anyone in my office.

Oh, this was too perfect. She'd be doing me in her office. If not today, soon.

Jana: Stop being so uptight. You need to let your hair down in more ways than one.

Zoe: Tell him I'm busy.

Jana: Absolutely not. Even if I did, he's not leaving. I can tell.

Zoe: Jana, how many times do I have to tell you my virginity isn't your concern?

Jana: Yes, it is. You're moody and you need to get it on with someone.

Me. She'd get it on with me. This little exchange only hammered home how ideal it was I happened to be around.

The office door opened and I quickly took a step back. Jana didn't need to find me craning my neck to be nosy. I couldn't fucking believe I'd just done that. It was safe to say I'd never even considered snooping to find out anything about a woman. That's how much I wanted Zoe. I shied away from pondering what that meant. All I knew was I wanted Zoe, and I'd have her.

Jana came around the corner and gestured to me. "Zoe had a cancellation. She'll see you now."

I don't know what Jana-my-favorite-person-today said but she'd obviously persuaded Zoe to see me. I happened to agree with Zoe that shagging her in her office probably wasn't the best plan. Once we took care of her pesky virginity, I'd be all over it. That said, I wasn't leaving today without another kiss and then some.

The door closed with a click behind me. For a flash, I considered locking the door, but I knew I had two hours, and I knew Jana wouldn't interrupt. Not after seeing what she just wrote.

I looked over to see Zoe standing by the windows. Her office looked out over downtown Seattle with Puget Sound visible past the skyline of buildings. Her back was to me, and I could see the tension in her spine. She stood straight with her arms crossed. She wore a fitted black skirt that fell just above her knees and another cropped jacket. This was a variation on what she'd been wearing every time I'd seen her. Always professional, always demure, and most definitely appropriate. I couldn't wait to shove that skirt up again. My mind instantly flashed to the way she looked the last time with her generous breasts spilling out of her blouse and her dusky pink nipples taut and damp.

Fuck me. The second I recalled that, blood shot straight to my groin. I gave my head a shake and walked to stand beside her.

"Hello luv. Were you going to ignore me much longer?"

Her cheeks turned pink, and she bit her lip. Oh hell. I needed to be in control if I wanted to play this right. Seeing her white teeth denting her plump bottom lip made me want to forget taking anything slow.

Her breath was audible. It came out in a ragged sigh. I could see her pulse beating wildly in her neck and wanted to dip my head and drag my tongue along the soft skin there.

She turned to face me, her arms still tightly crossed. What she didn't realize was doing that only served to push the plump curves of her breasts up. She was wearing a fitted camisole under her jacket. Dear God. Did she really think men didn't notice her? She walked around dressed like this all the time, and it was a temptation straight from hell because she somehow looked proper and insanely sexy all at once.

"I wasn't ignoring you. I was enjoying the view," she said crossly.

"Of me?" I couldn't keep from teasing because she made it all but impossible.

Her cheeks flushed deeper. Her mouth opened and closed and then she glared at me.

"No, Ethan. I wasn't enjoying the view of you," she said tightly, her voice carefully controlled.

I grinned. I bloody loved ruffling her composure. It kept me from feeling crazy about the effect she had on me.

I'd meant to come in here and start with asking her for an update since she had one for Coach. I also meant to take things slow with her. I might be a player, and I might like a good shag as much as the next guy, but I was bound and determined to make sure she had the best sex of her life since she was a virgin. As usual with Zoe, what I meant to do and what I did didn't line up.

I looked over at her—with her hair pulled back in another tidy knot without a single lock of that wild glorious auburn hair escaping, with her proper clothes, and with her mouth made for sin—and took one step, coming flush against her body. I startled her, and her arms fell apart when she gasped. I wasn't thinking. At all. I slid a palm up her spine and into her hair, promptly flicking the pins out and nearly groaning when her hair came loose. Long, wild waves of rich auburn fell around her shoulders.

"Ethan, what are you doing?"

Her voice came out raspy. About now, it occurred to me she might shove me away. But she didn't. She tensed, but she stayed right there. I was starting to get the idea she meant to hold her ground when she didn't back away like this. I'd seen her in action when she was in her working element—all confidence and no backing down. I figured it worked to my advantage just now. I could feel the beat of her heart against my chest and her rapid pants.

I didn't know what the hell I was doing, but I knew this —I would have her. All of her. Maybe not today, but soon.

"This," was my reply before I fit my mouth over hers.

She tensed against me, but when I swept my tongue in her mouth, she moaned and softened against me. Kissing her was like a fucking drug. I couldn't get enough. Once she let go, she kissed with abandon. Her tongue tangled with mine while her hands mapped my body. My cock was rock hard, and I couldn't get enough of her. I poured days of frustration into our kiss—hours and hours of replaying what it felt like to kiss her was nothing like actually kissing her. She flexed and arched against me as I kissed, licked and nipped my way down her neck.

Lust poured through my veins. I shoved her jacket out of the way, sending one button pinging against the window before it bounced to the floor. I couldn't say if her camisole was better or worse than her being bared to me. When I tore my lips from her skin—skin that tasted sweet and tangy at once—and glanced down to see her nipples straining against the silk, I groaned. I flicked my eyes up to her face. Her cheeks were flushed, her hazel eyes dark with need, and her lips parted as her breath came in these sexy little pants.

So much for control. I clung to the thinnest thread. My eyes on her, I loosened my hand where it had been tangled in her hair and dragged my finger down along her neck, tracing her collarbone and dipping down to circle one of her nipples —it was a tight little bead, begging to be touched.

Her breath hitched and a gasp escaped. My cock, already so hard I might've come just standing there, swelled a little more. I had to taste her. I traced up along the flimsy silk straps of her camisole and pushed them off her shoulders, shoving her camisole down until her breasts plumped over it. Yet again, I realized proper Zoe had a serious weakness for silk. Her bra was the sheerest silk imaginable with her dusky pink nipples easily visible.

I dipped my head and circled one and then the other with my tongue. She tunneled her hands into my hair and murmured my name. Did I mention I meant to take it slow? My intentions were pathetically weak when it came to Zoe. The moment she arched into me, I forgot what I meant to do. Everything blurred into the lust pounding through my body and the feel of her against me.

I drew away and flicked my thumb under the clasp between her breasts. The thin silk gave way and her breasts tumbled out. Tiny freckles were scattered here, there and everywhere on her skin. I wanted to follow where they led me. Palming her breasts, I let my lips meander wherever they wanted to go.

With her camisole shoved down and her skirt riding up as she twined around me, I cupped her bottom and yanked her to me as I drew a nipple in between my teeth again. The sounds she made drove me fucking wild. Breathy pants interspersed with husky moans. None of this was enough. I needed to taste more of her. Never once breaking my lips free from her skin as I toyed with her nipples, I maneuvered us away from the windows to her desk. Her hips bumped into it just as I dragged my tongue up along her neck. She gasped.

"Ethan, what... Oh my God. What are we doing? You have to..."

Her words ran out on a moan when I rolled a nipple between my fingers and caught her earlobe between my teeth.

I drew back. Hell, that made it seem like I was being a gentleman. I wasn't. At all. I needed to see every inch of her more than I needed to breathe. Just as powerful as that was the need to make sure she wanted this as much as me.

She was stunning. With her hair—fuck, her hair alone made me hard—tumbling down in a wild tousle around her shoulders, her skin flushed pink everywhere I could see, her lips swollen and her eyes dark with desire, she nearly brought me to my knees.

"Yes, luv?"

Her eyes slammed into mine. After a beat, she gave her head a little shake. Meanwhile, I trailed the backs of my fingers over the lush curve of her breast, savoring the hitch in her breath when I brushed over her damp, taut nipple. I beat back the urge to rush and kept going over the soft curve of her belly. Her bunched up skirt left her thighs— those glorious thighs—exposed to me. Her skin was like silk. I eased my hand under her bottom, a bottom she disguised quite well. Her skirts were so nondescript, you didn't notice she had a full, lush bottom. I could sink my hands into it and did just that as I lifted her and slid her onto her desk.

Right about now, I appreciated how tidy she was. Aside from her computer and phone in one corner and a few papers on a small table beside it, there was nothing else on her desk. She let out a gasp when I stepped between her thighs and arched into her. I could feel the wet heat of her through the silk and denim. She'd yet to reply to me.

"Luv, what was it you meant to tell me to do?"

Oh, perfect. Her gorgeous hazel eyes flashed. "We can't..."

Another low moan from her when I arched into her again.

"We can't what?"

"This, I told you. You're my client, and I can't..." She bit back a moan when I arched into her again. I couldn't keep this up, or I'd lose what little control I had.

"I'm your client, and I don't care, so that's a useless argument. Might I point out that it's quite obvious you're enjoying yourself?"

Her eyes flashed again. If she wanted to press the point, she elected against it. She held my gaze. The moment went from teasing to intense inside of a second. I could hardly breathe and wanted her so badly, it was a bloody miracle I hadn't taken things further yet. I'd lost all sense of time and had no idea how long it had been since I'd walked into her office.

She bit her lip. Oh hell. I was barely hanging on as it was, but she had to go and do that. She gave her head a shake and shocked me with a half smile. "I suppose I'd look foolish if I said I wasn't," she finally said. "I just think... Ugh. I don't do this kind of thing, and I'm not sure it's a good idea because I know I'm not the kind of woman you're usually, well, usually interested in. I already told you I'm a virgin, and I'm pretty sure that's a deal breaker unless you've lost your mind."

I could tell she was forcing herself to hold my gaze. Her chin tilted up, and her cheeks flushed a deeper shade of pink. When we weren't lost in each other, she started thinking. That didn't seem to be a good thing. I didn't like the uncertainty flickering in her gaze.

Annoyance flared. It chafed at me that Zoe didn't have a clue how amazing she was. Aside from the fact she was flat out gorgeous, she was brilliant to boot. That she'd try to compare herself to anyone and think she came up short, well, it rankled. It also chafed because I knew what she was getting at. I didn't particularly enjoy the media attention that came with my role, but I generally ignored it. Otherwise, it'd drive me bats. But I knew my alleged reputation as a player and had never minded it. I liked women, I liked fun, and I liked it with no strings attached. Zoe didn't fit the mold of woman I usually found myself with. Yet, I wanted her more than anyone and didn't like to hear her question that.

"I think it's bloody obvious you *are* the kind of woman I'm interested in. As for the other, I made it clear that was no deal breaker."

I meant my last comment to be teasing, but it came out fierce. Zoe's eyes widened, and her breath drew in sharply. She was quiet, the silence broken only by her shallow breath and the beat of my heart echoing through my body.

"Oh."

Her word fell into the quiet. Staring back at her, I lifted a hand and sifted it through her hair, my eyes drawn to how bright her hair looked against her bare shoulders where her skin was creamy and white and dotted with tiny freckles. I couldn't believe what came out of my mouth next.

"Do you want to stop?"

The air felt taut—weighted with desire and need. Inside my head, I couldn't believe I'd fucking asked that. Yet, once I did, I knew I had to. No matter how much I wanted her, and I was about out of my mind with need, I wasn't an asshole, and I wasn't going to push her past boundaries she didn't want to cross. She stared at me, her eyes searching mine. After a few beats, she shook her head the tiniest bit, shocking the hell out of me.

For maybe the first time ever, I was at a loss for words. I stared back at her, scrambling to gain a foothold in my mind —bloody hard to do when my cock was rock hard and nestled right against her damp heat.

With my heart beating out a wild rhythm, liquid need sliding through my veins and the heat of Ethan's hard cock against me, I could hardly argue I had the capacity to think. All I knew was what I wanted. *Him. More. Now.*

I should've entertained a few of the doubts that tried to shout their way into my conscience. But I'd apparently lost my mind because the desire clenching my belly tight overrode everything. My mind took a backseat to the sensation beckoning me.

When I shook my head, Ethan's eyes widened. He held still, his dark green gaze searching mine. Caught in his gaze like that, I felt exposed. The doubts I'd kicked to the curb got their groove back, and I started to feel restless. This was crazy. I started to wiggle back. His hand dropped from where he'd been toying with my hair and cupped my bottom, pulling me tight against his arousal again. Pleasure spiked through me, and I gasped.

"Okay then. Here's what I'm going to do," Ethan said, his taut voice sending shivers over my skin. "I'm going to make sure I don't leave this office until you're begging me for more. But there won't be more. Not today. We'll save that for later."

I should've thought he sounded cocky. I should've been mortified. I should've latched onto what little sense I had and found some way to untangle myself from him. Shoulda, coulda, woulda. None of that happened. His gruff, haughty voice left me leaning into the moment. I was flushed inside and out.

When I didn't say anything, his mouth curled at one corner before he dipped his head and nipped at my neck. What followed were the most intense, maddening moments I'd ever experienced. He proceeded to drive me wild with his hands, lips, teeth and tongue meandering down along my neck, over my breasts, teasing my nipples, and down over the curve of my belly. I was so wet, my panties were soaked and my thighs were damp.

He curled his hands over my hips and tugged me to the edge of my desk. In a distant corner of my mind, it occurred to me I had my skirt shoved up around my waist with my camisole shoved down to meet it. I wasn't just making out with a client, I was practically naked in my office on my desk and I didn't care. At all.

All I knew was I needed more than this. My channel was throbbing, and I needed release. As if he could see into the muddled, passion-addled haze of my mind, Ethan dragged his fingers over the silk between my thighs. A soft cry escaped and I arched into his touch. I didn't want any more teasing. In fact, I'd decided now was the ideal time to get rid of my pesky virginity. Right when I was about to speak up, he hooked his fingers over the edge of my panties and yanked them down. My hips lifted of their own accord and the black silk slid down my legs. I kicked them free and looked toward him.

His eyes had gone even darker, and his face was tense. I was awash in nothing but sensation and need and instantly restless from the brief interruption. Before my brain came online, his hands curled over my ankles and slid up my legs in one long, smooth, maddening stroke. The calloused surface of his palms lit fires under my skin and sent pleasure streaking through me.

He slowed to a stop at the juncture of my thighs, his eyes flicking up to mine. My hips shifted restlessly, and his eyes flicked down. Just when I thought I might die from need and melt into my desk, he eased one hand away and stroked his fingers through my folds. I was so close to release, I almost came right then. I couldn't hold back a ragged moan.

Ethan's eyes flicked up to mine and meandered down my body, striking sparks under my skin where they landed. Meanwhile, his fingers teased me, lightly dallying. My hips rolled into his touch, and his eyes whipped back to lock with mine.

The intensity of his gaze was too much, and I closed my eyes in reflex. I wasn't accustomed to being so out of control, so lost in nothing but sensation.

"Zoe."

My eyes flickered open. Just as I met his, he slid a finger into my channel, knuckle deep. I cried out, yet again so close to the edge of release, I almost tumbled over right then. I should've known only Ethan could drive me wilder.

Another finger joined the first. My hips bucked into the stroke of his fingers, and I gripped the edge of the desk to keep from sliding off. Next thing I knew, he brought his mouth to join his fingers. Dear God. His touch was wickedly, dangerously good. The exact right amount of teasing and pressure kept notching me higher and higher.

My channel clenched around his fingers as he drove inside me, while his tongue explored me so thoroughly I thought I might die from it. I kept thinking I'd topple over the edge, yet he kept pushing me right up to it and drawing back. I felt coiled tight inside. My hips rolled into him. Restless and needy, I murmured his name and begged him.

That's right, I *begged*. It did the trick when I gripped his hair with one hand. He swirled his tongue around my clit and sucked it into his mouth.

Pleasure uncoiled with a snap, whipping through me hard and fast. My channel throbbed around his fingers as he drove deep one last time. I felt him pull away and lift his head. I hadn't realized I was practically yanking his hair out until he moved. I loosened my grip and opened my eyes.

His hair was a rumpled, sexy mess thanks to me. I was pretty much useless. He held my gaze for a long moment and dipped his head to drop a few kisses right where my neck met my shoulder, promptly sending a shudder through me. Aftershocks of pleasure were still reverberating through me.

He straightened and slowly drew his hands away. I instantly missed his touch. He was quiet, exuding an intensity. I didn't know quite what to say as the reality of the moment sunk in. Next thing I knew, he'd snagged my panties off the floor and was sliding them up over my legs. In reflex, I shimmied off the desk, startled at how intimate it felt to have him tug them up over my hips and pull my skirt down.

He paused then, his eyes flicking up and back down. "I hate to make you cover your lovely breasts, but I suppose you have an appointment sometime this afternoon," he said, his voice coming out gruff and tense.

I don't know what I expected. I mean, what was I supposed to do when I'd gone flat crazy in my office? Ethan was solely responsible for any restraint we'd exercised. If he'd wanted to fuck me right there on my desk, I wouldn't have even tried to stop him. In fact, I was slightly let down he had.

My desk phone rang, which jolted me out of my haze. I looked to the phone and back to him. "Let it ring," he said softly.

I wasn't one to let a call go to voice mail when I was perfectly capable of answering. But Ethan had me transfixed, and I didn't want this moment to end. The phone kept ringing as he stepped away and gathered my bra and jacket before returning. The ringing stopped, and there was nothing but the soft rustle as he helped me back into my bra, pulled my camisole into place and settled my jacket over my shoulders. I was coming to realize why women chased after him with such wild abandon.

Aside from the fact he was devilishly handsome and a teasing flirt, he was dangerously good at driving me wild and now I was discovering he had a gracious, warm side, bordering on protective. It felt sublime, and if I were anyone other than me, I might've been able to let myself savor it more. As it was, I started to get uncomfortable with how good it felt. I had no idea how to navigate what had just happened. I might've been a virgin, but I wasn't untouched. I'd dated enough to have plenty of pretty heavy-duty makeout sessions. In all honesty, that had been far enough in my past that I couldn't recall anyone making me feel as Ethan just had—not even close. I did know with certainty, however, men didn't tend to appreciate one-sided pleasure unless the pleasure was theirs.

As far as I could tell, Ethan was planning to leave. He even hunted about for the button that had flown off my jacket and handed it to me.

"You should put your hair up."

His voice filled the quiet space and made me jump.

"I should?" I asked, slightly confused by it.

That dark look entered his gaze again. "Yes, luv. You should. I'd like to think only I get to see you like this," he said gruffly.

I'd later wonder why that didn't annoy the hell out of me. The ridiculous tendency for men to be high-handed usually chafed at me. I dealt with it so frequently in my professional life, I had a well-honed tendency to strike back at it. Yet, here and now with Ethan, I liked it. Alarm bells rang distantly in my mind. Next thing I knew, he strode over to the windows, his eyes scanning the floor, and returned with the two bobby pins that had held my hair in place.

"Are you leaving?" I asked, unsure what else to ask.

It didn't seem quite right to ask if he expected me to blow him. Nor was that the kind of thing that would sound right coming from my mouth. One look was all it took for me to know he was still plenty hard. His cock was outlined against his jeans.

He eyed me and nodded slowly. "I am. I'd like to stay, but I promised myself I wouldn't make your first time anything other than perfect. It won't be perfect on your desk with Jana just outside the door."

My eyes flicked down to his cock and back up. "But..."

He grinned. "I'm not a selfish man, luv. That you should know. Today was all about you. Now go put your hair up and then sit behind your desk and tell me about the message you left Coach Hoffman."

His sly grin sent my belly in a slow somersault. I bit my cheeks to keep from grinning right back at him. I was so utterly off kilter. Flustered, I spun around and ran my hands through my hair and swirled it up into a knot. I paused in front of the mirror on the wall and slipped the pins into place. My cheeks were flushed, my lips were swollen, and my eyes were bright. I looked as stunned as I felt. Somehow, I needed to get my shit together. Ethan was still here and had the ridiculous expectation I'd sit down and act like we were having a normal meeting.

With no other good idea of what to do, I surmised I might as well. I smoothed my skirt and turned, just then noticing I'd kicked off my shoes when I almost tripped over them. I slipped my feet into the simple black flats and strode behind my desk. Ethan was seated in the chair across from me. His expression was carefully bland, but I could see the gleam in his eyes and it made me flush. I ignored it and forced my gaze to my computer, quickly pulling up the email from the officer handling the charges related to the silly fight

Ethan had literally walked into. I'd admit to doubting him in the middle of the night when I went down to the police station, but I'd watched the security tapes myself. He had truly barreled right into the guy's fist.

I gave myself a shake and spun back to him. His dark green gaze was waiting for me. Our eyes locked and electricity sizzled through the air between us.

Chapter Eleven

ETHAN

I leaned my palms on the tiled wall of the shower and sighed. I'd somehow managed to keep myself from fucking Zoe right there on her desk, but bloody hell, it had taken every ounce of discipline I had. I'd meant it when I told her I didn't intend for her first time to be on a desk, but I was bound and determined we would christen it. I didn't remember much of anything she said after I asked her to fill me in on her message to Coach. I did remember the highlight, which was that the police were formally dropping the charges. After they'd had an opportunity to review all the security tapes, they decided either we were both charged, or no one was charged. Zoe had said something about how the fool who tried to get me charged could still try to sue, but my brain had been so fuzzed out I didn't remember much else.

I'd been torn because I didn't want to leave her office. Jana saved me when she knocked and announced Zoe's next client was arriving early. I'd practically run home, so I could take care of the raging hard-on I had. Now, I stood in the shower and wondered how the hell to stop obsessing about

Zoe. I let the scalding water pound down on my shoulders until it started to cool.

Toweling off, it occurred to me that all I'd managed to do was take the edge off of my out of control lust for Zoe. Hell, lust didn't even capture it. I knew without a doubt, once with her wouldn't exhaust my need. Not even close.

I dressed quickly and headed to the stadium. I needed to burn off my restlessness. I mentally sidestepped my discomfort. I wasn't used to thinking much about a woman the way I thought about Zoe. Oh, I loved women. I had no shame in how much I loved women. My sisters were forever on my case about how I needed to settle down, and they constantly teased about my reputation as a player. I didn't know what to make of the fact that I couldn't seem to even notice other women right now. On my walk to the stadium, I went out of my way to flirt with a woman who happened to be waiting at a cross street with me.

It was an utter failure. Don't get me wrong, she was gorgeous and she was interested. The failure was all on me. Beyond objectively noticing she was beautiful, I was entirely uninterested. Pure habit got me through teasing, but my heart wasn't in it. Then, I had to back my way out of an offer to meet her for dinner. So much for smooth.

I jogged down the stadium hallway to the locker room, changed into my workout clothes and set off for a grueling workout. I managed to exhaust myself, but Zoe was still lodged firmly in my brain.

A few days later after practice, Liam slid onto the bench in front of my locker. "Hey mate. You up for dinner tonight?"

I tossed my towel in the hamper in the corner and tugged a t-shirt over my head before glancing his way. "I'm always up for food. Who else is meeting us?"

"Dunno. Figured maybe we could snag Alex and Tristan."

I sat down across from him. "Where's Olivia?"

Liam was all but physically attached to Olivia at the hip

ever since he'd fallen for her. He used to run the circuit with me back in London. We'd hit up the pubs, have fun with women who were tagging along and carry on. Once we signed on with the Seattle Stars, he'd injured his knee and Olivia had been his surgeon. That was it. He was still one of my best mates, and I was damn happy for him, but it wasn't quite the same.

His piercing blue gaze met mine, and he ran a hand through his black hair with a sigh. "She's out of town all week at a conference. I feel like a bloody idiot because I hate going home when she's not there."

I couldn't help but laugh. He looked downright forlorn about the whole bit. 'You have Bentley to keep you company, right?" I asked, referring to their dog, a sweet, little brown dog that often napped in Coach's office during games.

Liam rolled his eyes. "Yes. Mate, you'll understand someday."

Zoe flashed through my mind. Truth was, she was almost always lingering along the edges of my thoughts.

"Right then. Let's go grab something. I'll round up Tristan. Where are we meeting?"

Relief washed over Liam's face, and he stood up quickly. "Great. I'll track down Alex. Let's meet out front."

In short order, I was seated at a table with Liam, Alex and Tristan. We saw each other almost daily, but with Liam and Alex settling down, we rarely spent time together like this anymore.

The evening ran its usual course except for one matter. Though it had been a good while since Liam had hitched up with Olivia and Alex with Harper, it only came to my notice tonight that I was the only one of us left who teased and joked about women. Usually. I didn't feel inclined right now, and it was all because of Zoe. Tristan might not be hitched to anyone, but the man treated sex like a purely mechanical task. He had some woman he saw here and there, but there were no strings attached whatsoever. I could hardly imagine him settling down with anyone. Though I'd have said the same thing about Liam and Alex before for different reasons.

After dinner, Tristan took off to meet the very woman he occasionally saw for what I'd guess was nothing but a good fuck. He never slept away from our flat. Me, I walked home alone in the drizzle. I'd grown to like Seattle, despite the frequency of rainy, gray weather. The streetlights glittered on the wet pavement. It had been a full four days since I'd seen Zoe, and I was mulling over how to see her again. It chafed at me that I wasn't being myself with her. I wasn't exactly a shy guy. Not I. If I wanted a woman, there were no games. I went at things quite directly. With Zoe, nothing seemed straightforward. I could always stop by her office again, but I wanted more than a make-out session in her office.

Somewhere along the way, I looked ahead and could've sworn Zoe was walking a block ahead of me. It was dark and rainy, but the streetlights cast enough light for me to recognize her long-legged stride. She had a bold, confident walk. Though my mind had threads of doubt, my body tightened in recognition. My stride picked up until I was almost jogging. As I got closer, any mental doubts as to whether it was Zoe disappeared. I slowed to a walk just before catching up to her.

"Hello Zoe," I said, striding to match hers.

She'd been walking with purpose and hadn't even turned to look my way when I reached her. She jumped a little when I spoke, and I suddenly realized I'd unintentionally frightened her. It was late and dark, and she was walking alone.

"Just me, luv," I added when her eyes caught mine.

Bloody hell. She was so hot. She hadn't bothered with a raincoat. Her hair was damp, and a lock had come loose from the usually tidy knot atop her head. It fell against her cheek. Raindrops glittered on her lashes.

"Oh, Ethan. What are you doing here?"

"Walking home. What are you doing?"

We stopped when we came to a cross street. She looked ahead and then back to me. "Walking home."

"Little late for you to be out, isn't it?" I couldn't resist a little teasing. It was all but impossible with her.

Her lips tightened, and her eyes flashed before she let out a heavy sigh. "I was just leaving work. Don't tell me you've been out to a bar? Your charges aren't officially dropped yet until it's cleared through court, so you need to behave."

This was perfect. She had that proper, uptight air that was like gas to a fire for me.

"No bar, luv. Just dinner with my mates. What are you doing working so late?"

Another sigh and another flash in her eyes.

"I work this late a lot."

"I bet you do. Let me walk you home." I hadn't planned to say what I said, but the second I did, my entire body tightened.

Traffic rolled past on the street and the drizzle fell softly around us. Zoe bit her lip and looked away. When she looked back to me, she gave a little shrug. "It's not far, but I guess if you want to."

I don't know what was passing through her mind, but uncertainty flickered in her eyes. I elected to ignore my own doubts and latched onto the chance she offered.

"It's late, it's dark, and it's raining. You shouldn't be walking alone." I hadn't meant to sound bossy, but I did.

Zoe arched a brow and straightened. I could see her spine go rigid. God, I fucking loved how easy it was to rile her.

"I walk home alone all the time. You know? Your high-handed act is ridiculous."

At that moment, the light changed and the traffic rolled to a stop. She looked ahead and began walking swiftly. I lagged for a beat, but I caught up. Once we reached the other side of the street, I reached for her hand. Because she was walking so quickly, I sensed she intended to shake me off. Her hand was icy cold when I slipped mine around it.

"Luv, you're freezing," I said just as she came to an abrupt stop.

My momentum from almost jogging to catch up to her sent me right into her. She stumbled slightly, and I reflexively reached to steady her. I hadn't planned it, but it was bloody perfect. She ended up flush against me. At which point I felt the fine shudder running through her. She was quite obviously cold.

The last thing I wanted to do was step back, but I had manners. I stepped back just enough to shake my jacket off and lift it over her shoulders.

"You don't need to do that," she protested, but she huddled into my jacket.

"Oh but I do. You're cold and wet."

She stood there, shivering and staring up at me. That loose lock of hair stuck to her cheek. I reached up and brushed it away, tucking it behind her ear. Her eyelashes glittered from the raindrops caught on them. In a flash, the air around us electrified.

I shackled the urge to kiss her because she was shivering, but I didn't intend to let this chance go. "Come, let's get you home." I slid my palm down her back as if I could somehow absorb her shivers and curled my hand around hers. "You were walking this way, so we'll keep going. Tell me where to go."

Her hand was icy cold in mine, but she didn't yank it away. "It's just a few blocks away," she said.

I didn't say aloud what I thought. She lived only minutes from the flat I shared with Tristan. We walked quietly through the rainy night. After another few blocks, she gave my hand a little tug and came to a stop.

"Here." She angled her head toward a small entryway to the side of a main entrance into a business.

"I'll walk you up," I announced, figuring she'd try to shoo me away.

She surprised me with a nod. "Your jacket's wet now. I'll throw it in the dryer for a few minutes before you go."

Obviously, that wasn't a problem with me. As I followed her through the entrance and up a flight of stairs to a hallway with echoing hardwood floors, I considered that what I wanted right now was to not leave here tonight without having all of her. I, so well known as a happy-go-lucky flirt who usually wanted nothing more than a good time, got nervous. Not about me, not about my performance, but about what it meant that I wanted Zoe the way I did. I'd never have argued that virginity was a deal breaker, but it held a sense of portent to it. I didn't usually go for anything of importance when it came to women and sex. In fact, I rarely slept—the sleeping kind of sleep—with any woman. Yet, I had it in my head I'd be waking up with Zoe after tonight and couldn't quite wait to see her sleepy with her hair down.

She wore tall boots that showcased her long legs. As usual, she also wore a fitted skirt—simple black and damp from the rain. For the first time, I considered the distance from her office to where I'd encountered her and realized she'd walked quite a way. It was no wonder she was chilled from the rain. Our footsteps echoed down the hallway. We passed several doors, and I gathered the upstairs of the business was flats. We reached the end of the hall when Zoe stopped and let go of my hand as she fumbled in her purse. As soon as she pulled her keys out, she dropped them.

Out of reflex, I leaned over to pick them up and handed them to her. Just that little touch sent a jolt of electricity zipping through me. Her eyes locked to mine. For a second, I didn't know what she meant to do. Then, she gave her head a little shake and turned to slide the key into the lock only to almost drop her keys again.

I curled my hand over hers. "Easy," I murmured.

The key slid into the lock and turned. The door swung open with a whisper. Zoe stepped away from me and walked across the darkened room to flick on a lamp in the corner. I closed the door behind me and glanced around. Her flat had high ceilings and hardwood floors, creating a spacious feeling though the flat was on the small side. We entered into the living room, which had a bright blue rug in the middle of the floor with a loveseat and two chairs flanking it facing a television mounted on the wall. The room was sparsely furnished beyond that. To the other side was a wide arched entry leading into the kitchen behind a counter with stools pushed against it. A short hallway was to the back of the living room. I surmised her bedroom and bathroom were back there.

Zoe returned to where I stood, resting a hand on the wall while she tugged off her boots. I didn't bother to ask and toed my shoes off as she removed my jacket from her shoulders and gave it a shake. The denim was soaked through at the shoulders. It probably had been when I handed it to her, but I hadn't noticed. She glanced to me. One look and my breath lodged in my throat for a beat. The tiny freckles dusted across her nose and cheeks stood out against her creamy complexion. With her hair damp from the rain, it was a deep, rich red. Her hazel eyes looked almost green in the muted light.

I was the guy who almost always found it easy to be smooth. At the moment, I was scrambling inside not to tear her clothes off, scoop her up and find the closest place to sink inside of her.

"I'll put this in the dryer," she said. "Okay?"

I managed a wordless nod and watched as she walked across the room and down the short hallway. She disappeared through a door, returning a moment or so later with the distinct sound of a dryer tumbling in the background.

She approached me, at which point I realized I was still standing by the door. Her eyes coasted over my face. I had no idea what she was thinking, but lust and longing were pouring through my veins and I was grasping about for what to do.

"Um, do you want something to drink?" she asked.

I shook my head, somehow latching onto enough of my usual cockiness to stop worrying. "I want you."

Her breath hitched and her cheeks went pink. I fucking loved it when she blushed. Bloody hell. This woman had me on my knees and she didn't even know it.

I decided then and there, I'd barrel ahead. If I didn't, I sensed she'd start thinking about it too much. I remembered her receptionist's teasing and guessed it meant she was letting her virginity get in the way of all kinds of fun. No matter how things played out with us, at least I could save her from letting that be a barrier anymore. A distant siren blared in my mind. Zoe wasn't just any woman, and my response to her was nothing of the usual for me. I didn't care to listen to the warning just now.

I closed the distance between us in two strides and lifted my hand to untie her hair. It fell in wet locks, the pins holding it up pinging on the floor. I sifted my fingers through, letting it spill around her shoulders. She was quiet, but her breath was shallow, and I could see the flutter of her pulse in her neck. I stopped trying to rein myself in and simply did what I wanted. I dipped my head and dropped kisses along her collarbone and up along the downy soft skin of her neck. Her skin was cool, and she tasted like rain tinged with sweetness.

"Ethan?"

The question in her tone had me lifting my head. "Yes?"

"I don't know..." She paused and bit her lip, her cheeks flushing deeper.

"Don't know what?"

She let out a heavy sigh and straightened her shoulders. "I don't know why you want to do this. I'm not the kind of woman..."

I gave my head a hard shake.

She eyed me. "Why does that make you angry? I'm not an idiot. If you're in the news, it's usually with some woman hanging onto you. Most of my life is about work. It's most of the reason I'm still a virgin. It's not because I'm uptight or anything. My career got in the way, and it's a nuisance if you ask me. My point is I'm not naïve or stupid. I know I'm nothing like the women you usually date."

I supposed the good thing about getting annoyed was I forgot to be worried about what any of this meant. I slid my palm down her back to slide over the curve of her bottom and pull her against me. I was rock hard. She gasped.

"That should be enough evidence for you," I murmured. For a beat, I waited to see if she'd pull away. When she didn't, I brought my lips right back to where they'd been on her neck—kissing, licking and nipping my way up to her mouth.

Chapter Twelve

ZOE

Ethan threaded a hand in my hair and fit his mouth over mine. The world felt like it was spinning as I tumbled into his hot kiss. Let me tell you, Ethan Walsh knew how to kiss like it was nobody's business. He alternated between devouring my mouth with deep sweeps of his tongue and drawing back to catch my lower lip in his teeth, swipes of his tongue across my lips, feathering kisses along my jawline and then finding his way back again. All in all, it's a damn good thing he held me against him because otherwise I'd have melted at his feet.

He drew back, his lips dusting along my neck to catch my earlobe between his teeth. Just that and hot shivers raced through me. My breath was choppy. I'd been chilled for the entire walk home and now the fire spreading through my veins in contrast made my skin prickle all over. It felt so good to be held against him—that alone was addictive. He moved with pure strength and ease, every touch smooth.

His breath gusted across my skin as he made his way down into the V of my blouse. A rough shiver ran through me, and he lifted his head.

"Still cold?" he asked, his eyes teasing and his mouth curling at one corner.

I glared at him, which only brought me a low chuckle and another shiver of heat rippling through me. Ethan moved swiftly and lifted me into his arms, swinging me so my legs hung over one of his forearms. I wasn't used to being carried. Being tall didn't exactly lead men to want to sweep me off my feet, so to speak. He held me easily. In a flash, I discovered it was pure heaven to be held against his muscled chest.

In his arms, my face was level with his. I glanced to him, and my heart started hammering. Dear God. He was ridiculously handsome. With his dark blonde hair, green eyes and chiseled features, it was no wonder women drooled over him. Throw in his roguish grin that he tossed about with abandon and a body to die for, and it was a near certainty I wasn't the only woman who got wet just being near him.

He started walking, aiming straight for the hallway at the back.

"Where are we going?"

"Bedroom."

"You don't even know where it is."

He glanced down, a devilish grin curling his lips. "Can't be too hard to find. There's only two doors back here," he said as he entered the short hallway.

A laugh bubbled up. I should've tried to stop this, but I didn't want to. I kept recalling Jana's point I was letting my virginity get in the way of any kind of dating. Twenty-nine wasn't that old, but it wasn't exactly young either. Seeing as I'd already almost gotten naked with Ethan, arguing with myself about crossing boundaries with him like this seemed pointless. If I was going to wave goodbye to my annoying virginity, I figured I could at least be guaranteed another phenomenal orgasm with him. Although I had my doubts he could top the one the other day in my office. I'd pretty much chalked that up to the best ever and figured it was a lucky break.

With the dryer rumbling audibly from the bathroom to one side of the hall, Ethan didn't even bother checking that door. He shouldered through my bedroom door opposite it and eased me down. I nudged the light switch with my elbow and adjusted the dimmer. I scanned the room, wondering how he saw it. My bed was a simple, low queen bed with a fabric-covered headboard. I loved pillows, so there were plenty of those, along with a fluffy down quilt. I spent many an evening propped amongst my pillows with my laptop on my knees as I drafted legal documents and reviewed case law. Beyond my bed, there wasn't much in the room. I had a giant walk in closet, which afforded enough space for a dresser.

I had turned away to flick on the lights and jumped when I felt Ethan's hands slide down my sides to hook over my skirt. For a flash, I froze. I didn't want to stop, I really didn't. But I didn't know what to think of the fact that I seemed to be barreling ahead into this. Ethan was the first man I'd kissed in over a year.

I'd tried here and there to fit dating into my too busy life. The last guy—a debonair finance attorney I'd met at a legal function—had seemed like a good bet. I figured he might actually understand my dedication to my work. I quickly learned he had skated by on charm both professionally and personally. He was mildly amused at my passion for my career and had no problem acknowledging he'd chosen finance law for the money. He'd also made it clear he had no interest in anything other than casual sex with no strings. While I'd be the first to admit my life didn't leave much room for a serious relationship, I wasn't running around looking to fuck all the time. Our first date came to a screeching halt when he jammed his tongue down my throat in the cab after our dinner date.

I spun to face Ethan, just as he paused. I could tell he

sensed my hesitation. Ugh. I hated this. This was precisely why I was annoyed I'd focused so hard on studying during college. I hadn't meant to end up a virgin at twenty-nine, most certainly not. It would have been much easier to lose it in a drunken night of partying in high school or college, like so many friends I knew. Not me though. It wasn't that I judged those who chose to party like that, but I'd had goals and I didn't let anything get in the way.

I opened my mouth to speak, but since I didn't know what to say, I snapped it shut. His hands were warm against my waist. He eyed me, his teasing gaze fading.

"This doesn't have to go any further," he said suddenly. "I might want you like mad, but nothing happens that you don't want."

If I knew anything with certainty, it was this—I wanted Ethan, I wanted this, and I didn't want to stop. Those thoughts galvanized me. I shook my head forcefully.

He stared at me. "You're going to have to be clear, luv. I don't know if you're shaking your head because you don't want this, or something else."

"I want you. I want this," I said, the words coming out fiercely, rough and raw between my ragged breathing and racing pulse.

His gaze darkened. "Okay then."

He curled his fingers over the waistband of my skirt and slid it over my hips. It fell in a quiet rumple around my feet. As I kicked it out of the way, he set to undoing the buttons on my blouse.

"Let's get these pesky clothes out of the way first," he murmured, his voice sending a prickle up my spine.

I was still slightly chilled from my rainy walk home. When the cool air drifted against my skin when my blouse fell open, I shivered. Little did I know that would lead to Ethan moving like lightning. In a flash, my blouse was tossed aside. Before I had a chance to form a thought, he peeled off his shirt.

One look and my mouth watered. It wasn't like I didn't know he was cut. But... Oh. My. God. He probably missed his calling and should've been a model. His skin was like caramel and every inch of his chest and abs was muscle. He had the lightest dusting of gold hair on his chest that narrowed down to a point past the waistband of his jeans. Which I *really, really* wanted him to take off. He obliged in a matter of seconds. The rest of him was just as yummy as his chest. There couldn't have been an ounce of fat on him. He was nothing but lean and muscled everywhere I looked. His fitted black briefs did nothing to hide his blatant arousal.

Mere seconds had likely passed since I'd shivered, but with Ethan nearly naked in front of me, I wasn't thinking too clearly and had completely forgotten I was chilled. He hadn't however. In a flash, he'd tugged me to the bed and was stretching out beside me. He was like my own personal furnace, and it was simply delicious. I could've burrowed into him and been perfectly happy to stay there for days. He was warm all over, his skin sleek and hot.

In a matter of seconds, my chill was chased away as he began mapping my body with his hands and mouth. I went from being cold, damp and tired after a long day at work to so hot and bothered, I could barely think. I tumbled into the headiness of being with him. Fire roared through my body, and liquid need throbbed at my core. I couldn't get close enough and was busy greedily touching him every-where I could. He paused with his lips between my breasts and flicked his thumb under the clasp of my bra. My nipples tightened further at the feel of the cool air against them when the silk slid away.

He glanced up, his eyes hooded, before dipping his head and swirling his tongue around a nipple. I moaned when he closed his mouth over it and bit down lightly. He settled his weight over me—oh my god, it felt good—and set to make me wild. He kissed, licked, sucked and nipped at both of my breasts, blowing softly when he drew away. All the while, I could feel every inch of his hard, hot length against my core through the layers of his briefs and my silk panties. Pleasure spiked through me with every subtle shift of his body against mine.

His weight shifted as he made his way down my body, dusting kisses over my belly and pushing my knees apart. I was fairly certain I could now conclude it was possible to climax without a single touch where it was supposed to matter. That's how far gone I was. I could feel the moisture between my thighs, and my channel was throbbing. When he dragged a finger across the wet silk, my hips bucked and I almost came. I didn't think I could take much more.

"Ethan..." I murmured on the heels of a moan.

"Hmm, luv?" he murmured in return, his lips against the sensitive skin on the inside of my thigh sending another jolt of pleasure to my core.

"I need..."

My words ran out when he curled his hand over the edge of my panties and dragged them off swiftly. Before I could catch my breath, his fingers were sinking inside of me and his mouth was on me. With his fingers teasing and stretching me and his tongue tracing wickedly around and over my clit, it was a matter of seconds before my climax wracked me. I came in a noisy burst with shudders rolling through my body with such force, I was nearly limp when they subsided.

Ethan slowly drew away, and I instantly missed the feel of him when he leaned off the bed. He snagged his jeans. Confused, I looked up to see him kicking off his briefs and tugging a condom out of his wallet, which fell to the floor with a thump when he tossed it aside. Of course, his cock was as perfect as the rest of him. I'd had a sense he was well-endowed, but the sight of him gave me a flicker of anxiety. Overriding that anxiety was the yearning to feel him inside of me. It didn't matter that I'd just had an explosive orgasm, all I could think about was how much more I wanted.

He stretched out over me again, his weight to the side. He brushed my still damp and tangled hair away from my face, his gaze going somber. "Now would be the time to tell me you want to stop," he said, his voice taut, but clear.

I shook my head, and his mouth curled at one corner. "Luv, I don't know what that means. You'll have to tell me."

My heart felt tight in my chest, and a flash of uncertainty rose inside. I wasn't uncertain about this moment. No, it was the feelings Ethan elicited. I kept expecting him to be cavalier and to behave like the player he was portrayed to be in the media. Yet, he wasn't that way with me. Even when he was teasing and flirting and trying to get under my skin, he wasn't mean-spirited or cavalier. I'd have expected him to look at me as a conquest to be had, but that's not how I felt. Not at all. Beyond the hot rush of pleasure at simply being with him, every moment felt incandescent—lit with an intimacy that shimmered around and between us.

He arched a brow, and I realized I hadn't answered. With my heart beating wildly and heat rolling through me, I swallowed and found my voice. "I don't want you to stop." My voice came out rough and raspy. Inside I felt hot, liquid and needy. All I wanted was him to stop talking and sink inside of me.

"What do you want?" he murmured, his eyes still on me.

My heart tripped and my belly executed a slow flip. He wasn't going to let me do anything other than make it perfectly clear. "I want you," I finally said over the thundering beat of my heart.

He held my gaze for another moment before nodding, His eyes dipped down, everywhere they landed sending slivers of pleasure under the surface of my skin. In a flash, he rolled on a condom and eased his weight atop me. He met my gaze again. Something between concern with a hint of uncertainty flashed in his gaze. I could feel his cock against me. I was slippery wet and the feel of it hot and hard there sent little shocks of pleasure through me. I was restless and didn't want to drag this out. I dragged my tongue along his neck—he tasted salty with a hint of the rain we'd walked through.

He curled his palms in mine and adjusted his hips before pausing. That wouldn't do. I wanted this part done and over with. I curled my legs around his hips and arched into him. I should've known he wouldn't let me run this show. He held still, although his cock sank a little further inside.

"Zoe," he murmured, his voice dark.

I lifted my head from where I'd been meandering up his neck. "Hmm?"

"Let's not make this worse than it needs to be." His features were tight, and I sensed he was holding on by a thread. So I endeavored to snap it.

"Let's get it over with." I spurred a heel into his buttock, which was nothing but muscle and barely even dented.

He chuckled and eased a little further inside. Only then did it start to burn. I was all about barreling through it, so I arched into him the next time he sank further in. On the heels of burning pain, he surged inside of me to the hilt and held still. My body had tensed in reflex, and my breath hissed.

"Are you okay?" he asked, his voice tight.

"Uh huh," I managed with a nod. I was. It was tight and he barely fit, but the pain was already easing.

Without a word, he dipped his head and started dusting kisses along my neck and over my breasts. Between a few moments and the delicious distraction, the burning sensation faded and my body relaxed again. Somewhere along the way between kisses and nips that sent shivers all over, he began to move, setting a slow, easy pace. The effect was only to drive me wild with need. With every stroke, my channel clenched around him. I was hot all over and caught up in chasing after another release.

Once the pain faded, the delicious stretch of him inside me felt so good, it was like a drug. I tumbled into nothing but sensation, the pull and slide of him inside of me, his hands gripping mine, and his eyes burning into me. Pressure spun tighter and tighter until he freed one of my hands and reached between us. Just a swirl of his thumb on my clit and pleasure burst in a ray through me. Shudders hit me so hard, I could barely breathe. I felt him tighten and cry out roughly before he relaxed against me. He shifted his weight to my side, which I didn't like. I wanted him fully inside of me and every inch of him against me.

"Why'd you move?" I asked between heaves.

His low chuckle reverberated through my body. "I don't want to crush you."

I opened my eyes to find his teasing gaze waiting. My heart tripped again and my breath hitched, but I kept my head. "I'm too big. You won't crush me."

Another chuckle reverberated. "Ah, excellent point. Okay, I shall take that as permission to crush you whenever I want."

My chest felt tight and a rush of emotion rolled through me. I didn't know what it was about what he said, but it made me feel funny and want things I didn't expect to want with anyone, much less with Ethan.

Chapter Thirteen

ETHAN

The subtle glide of silky skin against my leg woke me. For a beat, I was disoriented, my mind hazy from sleep. The warm body curled against me was puzzling and then my brain came back online. Zoe was draped over half of my body. I couldn't help but grin. One of her legs was curled over mine with her foot tucked between my calves. With her head resting against my shoulder, her palm on my chest and my hand curled under her and cupping her bottom, I could feel all of her lush curves against me. This had to be about the best way to wake up. Ever. I'd never considered what I was missing by always skipping out after sex. Of course, this was Zoe and that made it all the better. I'd yet to even care to think about waking up beside someone. After last night, you'd have needed physical force to get me out of her bed.

Her breathing was steady and even, gusting softly against my shoulder. I'm not sure if my cock was hard when I was asleep, but it was now. I couldn't recall waking up hard since I'd been a randy adolescent. My mind spun back to last night. My early mental gymnastics about being responsible for Zoe waving goodbye to her virginity had turned out to be a waste of mental energy. I couldn't have guessed how bloody amazing it would be to be with her though.

If my body had its say right now, I'd roll her over and sink right back inside of her. Yet, I didn't think that was the wisest idea, given she was likely sore. There was that and the fact I hadn't a clue what to do with my feelings. *Feelings*. Not something I thought much about. Oh, I cared about people. My mates were like family to me, and I'd do anything for them. I'd take a bullet for my sisters and my mum and dad. But the whole idea of seriously being involved with a woman had never occurred to me. I was too busy having fun. I'd watched Liam fall like a rock falls from the sky for Olivia and chalked it up to random chance. Liam and I had once been far more alike when it came to women. He was a free-wheeling playboy until Olivia came along. Now here I was with Zoe curled against me and feeling like my heart had tripped and fallen on its ass. I had to wonder what was in the water here in the States.

I started to get uncomfortable, so I tried to shut my bloody mind up. Problem was, Zoe was beside me, warm and tempting beyond all reason, and I wanted her like mad. Last night hadn't done a bit to tamp down my pure lust for her. Rather, it had been like octane fuel to a fire that was already raging. She shifted in her sleep again and her breathing altered. I sensed she was awake, but I knew it when she lifted her head.

The light filtering through the shades in her bedroom was wispy gray. It had the effect of making her auburn hair seem brighter and her hazel eyes stood out against her creamy skin. With her hair rumpled from sleep, all it took was one look and blood shot straight to my already hard cock. As she stared at me, her cheeks flushed. I loved it when she blushed. That's all she had to do and I was pretty much useless. Bloody hell. If she had any idea the effect she had on me, I was doomed.

The air around us heated as if lit by a flame all of the

sudden. When we'd fallen asleep last night after a shower, I'd figured it would be nice to wake up with her and we'd have tea or coffee or something like that. I hadn't counted on this —this fiery need coming to life the moment we were both awake.

I'd imagined how she'd look sleepy, but my imagination was an utter failure. Her tousled auburn hair, her rosy cheeks, the dusting of freckles on her skin and the feel of her lush body against mine—all of it together felt so fucking good I could hardly breathe. Throw in the way it felt to look in her eyes—unguarded, she was breathtaking. My heart set to thudding against my ribcage as awareness scored me.

I could feel her heart beating against my side, the pace kicking up as we lay there. She bit her lip. Fuck me. When she did that and her teeth dented her plump bottom lip, it made me crazy. The good kind of crazy, but still. I had to remind myself I absolutely could not plan on burying myself inside of her right now, no matter how badly I wanted to. I was no virgin expert, but I had some sense and knew she must be sore.

She cleared her throat, the sound breaking through the weighted quiet. "How long have you been awake?" she asked, her voice husky from sleep.

I began to wonder if there was anything she could do that didn't turn me on more. I forced my mind to her question, simple enough to answer.

"A few minutes. Good morning," I replied, unable to keep from grinning when the pink on her cheeks deepened. Hell if I knew why she blushed so often, but I fucking loved it.

She bit her lip again. Oh, that was it. I slid my palm off her bottom—hard to do by the way—and up her spine to tangle in her hair. There wasn't much space between us, so it took just the slightest movement to bring her mouth to mine. I wasn't thinking—not at all—and the moment she sighed against my mouth, I slipped my tongue between her lips and poured the need burning hot and high inside of me into our kiss. She tensed against me for a beat, but when I slid my hand back down her spine and nudged her atop me, she relaxed. Our kiss went wild. Mentally thrown and emotionally disoriented by the effect she had on me, I flung myself into the heat of the physical moment between us. I latched onto it as if it were the only thing that could ground me. Meanwhile, I was like a train running off the tracks, barely hanging onto any semblance of control.

The feel of her full breasts pressed against me and her slick folds sliding over my cock—because it was that perfect when her knees fell to the sides of my hips—nearly made me forget my promise not to bury myself inside of her post haste. When my fuzzy thoughts turned to clambering away from her to find a condom, reality nudged me, hard enough I rolled us over quickly.

That didn't help matters. At all. Now, my cock was nestled against her drenched core, and all I wanted to do was adjust my hips and sink inside. Condom or no, I had to get myself out of the danger zone. I shimmied down her body, probably a touch rougher than I should be with my lips, teeth and tongue as I made my way down. Bloody hell though, she didn't help matters between her breathy pants, husky moans and her hands all over me. The moment I sucked one of her nipples into my mouth, I managed to get my mind off of what it would feel like to be inside of her again. Fuck. She tasted so good and when she buried her hands in my hair and arched into me, I sank my teeth in before pulling back to look at her.

Her hair spilled over the pillows, stark and bright against the white. Her hazel eyes were a dark swirl of gold, green and brown, and her lips were red and swollen. Her nipples were damp and taut from my attentions. With her breath rising and falling rapidly, she arched into me, starting to curl those long legs around me. Uh oh. I had to keep moving. I tore my gaze from hers and mapped my way down her body, kissing, licking and nipping my way over the soft curve of her belly.

I pushed her knees apart and almost groaned at the sight of her. Her folds were pink and swollen. I meant to ask if she felt okay, but she buried her hands in my hair. With the core of her mere inches away, consideration lost the war in an instant. I dipped my head and dragged my tongue along her cleft. The salty tang of her was an unholy temptation and I lost myself in exploring every inch. I sank a finger inside and felt her clench around me and tense. Finally, fucking finally, my mind shouted above the raw lust pounding through me.

I drew back, and my breath lodged in my throat for a beat. She was glorious. With her skin flushed all over, those freckles that made me crazy scattered like constellations about her body, and her hair a tangled mess, it was a bloody good thing I wasn't standing or she'd have brought me to my knees in more than the figurative sense. As it was, I had to give my head a shake to recall she'd tensed. My finger was still buried knuckle deep inside of her.

"Are you okay?" I managed to ask, my voice taut with the need thundering through me.

Her eyes widened, and she arched her hips into my touch, nodding vehemently. If anything, she looked annoyed with me as if I was an idiot for even asking. I couldn't help but grin because that's what happened when she was annoyed with me. "Just checking, luv," I replied before getting right back to business.

With her legs curling around my shoulders and her hips bucking into my mouth, I fucked her with my fingers and tongue for much less time than I wanted. Within moments, she was tensing and murmuring my name in a noisy burst, her channel clenching and throbbing.

In a very short time, I'd discovered Zoe was rather expressive when it came to sex and didn't hold back at all. I eased away and started to kiss my way back up her body, but she dislodged me. She was tall enough to throw me off, and she did just that, promptly sitting astride me again. Just like that, all of my control slipped until I was clinging to its edge with my fingertips. She didn't give me much time to think and before I knew it, she was kissing her way down my chest and abdomen and curling a palm around my cock.

I don't know what I expected, but I certainly didn't expect to be given the best blowjob of my life by a woman who'd been a virgin less than twelve hours ago. Alas, that's precisely what happened. She had a wicked mouth and tongue and had me gripping the sheets as if my life depended on it. I was as close to the edge as she'd been, so the moment she drew me fully into her mouth, I was almost there. With her tongue swirling and the hot, wet suction around my cock, my release hit me with a roar and I spent myself in her mouth.

Stunned, I fell back into the pillows as she slowly drew away and wiped the back of her hand across her delectable mouth that had just now shown me the peaks of its naughtiness. She eased up beside me and fell into the pillows, half draped over me. All the while, I was wondering if I could ever get enough of her. I should've been spent, instead all I could think of was what was next.

Chapter Fourteen

ZOE

I looked across my desk at Jana and bit back a laugh. We were on a conference call with another law firm, actually the same firm representing the idiot who'd punched Ethan, and Jana was making faces at the phone. I leaned forward and tapped the mute button.

"Stop it! You're going to make us both laugh," I hissed.

Jana rolled her eyes and brushed a lock of purple-streaked hair out of her eyes. "Why are you whispering? You muted the speaker."

I shook my head and gave into the urge to laugh. "Point taken. Oh my God. Ted loves to hear himself talk. I swear he's talked for about ten minutes on the same point."

Jana gave the phone another eye roll. "That's his thing. Yawn. He annoys the hell out of me. Why do so many people hire him?"

"Because he knows how to market," I said with a shrug. "We could probably learn a thing or two from him."

Now Jana glared at me. "No. We're not plastering billboards with your picture all over the place. It's so cheesy." She paused and twirled a lock of hair around her finger, eyeing me thoughtfully. "On second thought, maybe we should. You're totally hot. I bet we'd get a ton of new clients that way."

I tossed a paper clip at her, which she deftly caught and promptly returned to my desk. "I'm plenty busy. I don't need to work more anyway. You're always on my case for working too much."

She grinned. "True. But if we had more clients, you could hire more paralegals, instead of just me being your lonely paralegal slash receptionist. If we found some good ones, they could do all the grunt work and you could work less. Plus, you can't tell me anymore you're not hot. Ethan Walsh, practically the hottest ticket in town, totally has it bad for you."

Just when I was about to mouth right back at her, Ted said my name, loudly enough I realized we'd probably lost track of the conversation. Fortunately with Ted, we could gloss over that pretty easy. I tapped the button to unmute the phone and jumped back into legal mode.

Later that day after a slew of meetings, Jana came into my office and plunked down in the chair across from me. For days, every time I had a minute to think, my mind went straight to Ethan. Just now, I looked across my desk and recalled he'd made me come right there on my desk with his wicked mouth and fingers. I gave my head a little shake and focused on Jana.

"What's up?" I asked as I hit send on an email and looked over at her.

"It's the first time in three days we've had time to talk. Yesterday I wasn't here and today's been nuts. Fess up. What happened with Ethan? Don't try to tell me nothing because I saw how you looked after he came out of here last week, and I might've seen a text from him on your phone earlier."

My cheeks got hot. I wanted to be annoyed with her, but it was half-hearted. I latched onto the phone thing because it was an easy target. "Since when have you started snooping on my phone?"

"Since you left it sitting right in front of me while we were suffering through Ted's monologue," she retorted. "I didn't see what it said, just his name. What did it say?"

Ethan had taken to texting me like crazy. I didn't know what to make of it, but I secretly liked it. A lot. He alternated between asking about my day, wanting to know how I was doing and flirting so brazenly, it made me hot all over just from reading a text. It wasn't that I hadn't dated. It's just that it had been a while, and it had never been all that great. I'd figured losing my virginity would be more like finally taking care of a chore I'd been blowing off. I was entirely unprepared for the burning hot intimacy I'd experienced with him, and the fact it was seared into my body, heart and mind so deeply tiny reminders of him sent heat rolling through me all over again. I gathered my nerve, shoved away my embarrassment and looked over at Jana.

She'd endured private and public humiliation over her unbeknownst-to-her affair, and she'd managed to pick up the scraps of her dignity and carry on just as boldly as before. I could handle being a little embarrassed about the fact I had no idea what to do about Ethan.

"We had sex. I have no idea what to do and he keeps texting me and telling me he wants to have dinner," I blurted out in a run-on sentence without a single breath in between words.

Jana's eyes widened. She watched me for a moment before her surprise melted into concern. "Hey, don't look so worried. It's perfect. You finally ditched your virginity, and he likes you. I'd have considered it a win if you got it on with him once, but it sounds like he wants more than that. Let me see the texts," she said, wagging her fingers at me. "I'm guessing you need some interpretation."

Relieved, I gladly handed my phone over. She knew the password, just as I knew hers, and promptly keyed it in.

After a minute of scrolling through my texts, she looked up. Her blue eyes were wide and her mouth fell open.

"What? Why do you look like that? I don't know what to do and he keeps texting and..."

Jana recovered and let out a whoop. "Zoe. He likes you. He *really* likes you. This is so awesome." She actually teared up as she looked over at me.

"Oh my God. Why are you getting all emotional? You don't even know if..." My words floundered as a sense of confused panic scurried through me. I felt buffeted by my emotions, which were all but flying loose as a leaf scuttles and spins in the wind. I was used to feeling calm and in control, and I couldn't find the center to hold onto when it came to Ethan.

She threw a glare at me. "I might've been stupid enough to have an affair I didn't know I was having, but aside from that fiasco, it's fair to say I've had more experience with men than you. Trust me, guys don't send texts like this if they don't like you. He's texting you at least four or five times a day telling you boring shit about his day and asking all about yours. He's flirting and he keeps asking you to dinner. Why the hell don't you just go to dinner, instead of making excuses like you've been doing?"

I opened my mouth to reply, but she held her hand up. "Hang on. The reason I'm getting all emotional is because you're fucking awesome. You're one of the nicest, smartest women I know. I respect the hell out of you professionally and did long before you hired me. You're one of the few people from law school who didn't look down their nose at me for being stupid about everything that went down. Whether you want it or not, you deserve a guy who appreciates you for who you are. I knew when Ethan came in to meet you that first time that he had a thing for you. Maybe he has a rep as a player, but he's not treating you like that. That's why I'm emotional. You deserve something other than a great career. I don't know what might happen with Ethan, but it's off to a smoking start."

She slid my phone back across the desk to me. If I hadn't caught it, it would've fallen to the floor. "Text him back right now and tell him yes to Friday."

My jaw went slack as I stared at her. My belly clenched and my pulse shot off again. Anxiety tightened my chest, and I didn't know what the hell to do. Part of me was elated at everything Jana said, yet I was also terrified. I didn't like feeling tossed about inside like this, and nothing seemed to help. My boring life seemed so appealing compared to this emotional rollercoaster. I gave myself a shake.

"Jana, that Friday thing is like a *thing*. I can't go to a friends thing with him," I protested.

"Why not? It's less intense than something one on one."

I eyed her with my belly doing little flips just thinking about seeing Ethan again. I wanted to say yes. Hell, it's a miracle I hadn't said yes to every time he'd asked. It had been four days since I woke up beside him, and he'd reliably asked me to see him in some form every day since. Even though it made me nervous, Jana had a point. Seeing him in a group might be a little less nerve wracking.

She still had her wide blue eyes pinned to me with a brow arched. I could feel the silent dare.

"Fine. I'll say yes to Friday." I snagged my phone and opened the text.

"Why wait? See him tonight, so you can screw his brains out once more. You'll be more relaxed that way," Jana interjected with a sly grin.

I had to admit it was tempting. So, so tempting. But I didn't know how much of Ethan I could handle, especially when I longed to see him again and got wet just thinking about it.

I glared at her. "Friday. I'm doing Friday."

"No, you're doing Ethan."

I threw another paper clip at her and texted Ethan while Jana's laugh followed her out of my office.

Ethan's reply was swift.

Perfect. I'll meet you at your place at 6. What about tonight?

I'm busy.

I'd never been great at manufactured excuses. I could always be busy because there was always work to do in the evenings, poring over case law and preparing legal documents. So my answer was true, although it left out the fact that my mind was stuck on an endless loop of Ethan when I wasn't totally focused on something else.

If you hadn't just told me you'd have dinner tomorrow, I'd think you were avoiding me.

Oh, he knew how to get under my skin.

I am NOT avoiding you!

Perfect. Then you won't mind me stopping by your office in a few. On my way up right now. ;)

Gah! I threw my phone down and then froze. What the hell was wrong with me? I resisted the urge to run and check my appearance in the mirror. It had been a long day, and I knew I probably looked a little worse for the wear. But I would *not* start acting like an idiot all over a man. While I had a stern little chat with myself, my belly clenched and I got flushed just knowing I'd be seeing Ethan any second now.

My phone buzzed and I tapped the speaker. It might not be him, so I needed to act normal.

"Yes?"

"Ethan Walsh is here to see you," Jana replied cheerily.

I could feel the sly joy in her voice. I forced myself to play it cool because I knew he could likely hear me. "Thank you. I have a few minutes free," I said, keeping my voice level.

The speaker clicked off and I stood and walked to the windows, restless and about to jump out of my skin. I heard the door open and close with a click, but I forced myself to keep looking out the windows. I didn't quite know what to do about the effect Ethan had on me. It was beyond ridiculous, and I was starting to feel more than a little foolish. I was used to not noticing men, which was much easier for me. Knowing what I knew of him, I knew he was accustomed to women throwing themselves at him. I didn't want to be as consumed as I was by my desire for him.

His footfalls were muted on the carpet, and I felt him come up behind him. My body was drawn like a magnet to his—I could feel the heat of him before he reached me. I jumped when his hands slid down my hips and he dipped his head to drop kisses along the side of my neck. His touch was like a flash of fire roaring through me.

"So you're not avoiding me, luv?"

Oh. My. God. How the hell was I even supposed to think I could get control of myself when this was how he greeted me? His question was a murmur against my neck, the subtle motion of his lips on my skin sending a prickle of heat down my spine.

I swallowed, wrestling mightily to get control of my body. It was no use. I melted against him when his arms slipped around my waist, one palm coming to rest just above the apex at my thighs. I could already feel the wetness between my thighs. All I wanted was to feel him inside me again.

"I must've missed your answer," he murmured before he nipped at my ear, sending a ripple through me.

Sweet hell. I might as well have given up right then and there. I wanted Ethan so much it made me crazy. I clung to what little control I had and cleared my throat.

"I'm not avoiding you. I've just been..." My voice cracked when he slid a hand up and palmed a breast, lazily drawing his thumb back and forth across my nipple, which was taut and all but begging aloud to be touched. "Busy," I finally managed on the heels of a gasp.

I scrambled to get control of my body, but then he slid his other palm down to cup my mound, exerting a subtle pressure over my clit. A little moan escaped, and there was nothing I could've done to stop it. "Ethan, you can't..."

My words trailed off again. Really, what was I supposed to do? With his lips hot on my neck, his hands teasing me to madness and his hard, hot cock nestled against my bottom, I was pretty much a slave to him whether he knew it or not.

He lifted his head. "Can't what?"

Before I managed to form words to reply—because it wasn't easy with my brain all but mush—he reached up and deftly slid the pins out holding up my hair.

"You should wear your hair down more often," he said, his voice gruff as he sifted his fingers through it and turned me in his arms.

I met his dark green gaze, and my heart clenched while my belly executed a slow flip. Somehow I managed to answer his question over the need roaring through my body.

"I thought you said I shouldn't let anyone else see it down."

His mouth curled at one corner, a devastating grin that pierced me through. "So I did. I've reconsidered. I'd like to see it down more often, so I don't mind sharing."

A laugh bubbled up. I should've been affronted, but I wasn't. Not even a little. A buzzy joy rose inside to think he noticed me that much.

His grin stretched to the other corner of his mouth, his dimple making one of its appearances and sending my belly in another flip. His grin faded as his eyes dropped and he toyed with the ends of my hair.

"I only have a few minutes. We have a game tonight. I might've detoured a few blocks to see you."

"Oh? You didn't have to do that."

His eyes swung back up to meet mine. "If I wanted to see you I did."

I didn't know quite what to say, so I stuck with the concrete. "If you have a game, when were we going to have dinner?"

Another half grin from him. "Ah. You are a woman of detail. Truth is, I meant to chase after you and pester you until you said yes. I lost track of what day was what."

That teasing manner that came so easily to him. He was utterly unabashed at admitting he was chasing after me. Given he was a man who could probably have his pick of women, I didn't know what to make of that. It made my insides feel funny and made me hot all over.

"Oh. Well then, I guess tomorrow works better then," I managed over the pulse pounding in my ears.

"Unless you want to come to the game," he said.

I don't know why, but that startled me. His eyes were hopeful, and I found myself nodding. "Okay. I've never been to a soccer game. What time do I go?"

My answer seemed to surprise him as much as it did me. His eyes widened and then narrowed. "It's football, luv."

He seemed so affronted, I laughed, but then he slid a palm down my back to curl over my bottom, bringing me flush against him. The hard heat of his cock was impossible to ignore. He carried on as if we were having a casual conversation, while I thought I might melt on the spot.

"I'll let it slide since you're American. Anyway, the game's at six. If you come around five, I can introduce you to Olivia. She's Liam's wife. She'll take you up to the box with her. Any other way, and it might take some doing to get you in without a ticket this late."

My eyes flicked to the clock on the wall above the door. It was four o'clock now. Again, my body seemed to be running the show. I was nodding before I realized it.

"Okay, where do I go?"

"Please tell me you know where the stadium is," he said with a look of trepidation in his eyes.

"I know where that is. Give me some credit."

He grinned again. "Right then. Go around back to the entrance there. I'll tell security to look for you. I'll do my best to meet you there, but it depends on a few things. I promise Olivia will wait for you. You'll like her," he said firmly.

I knew who Olivia was only because I'd seen her picture here and there in the media when she attended functions with Liam Reed, another one of the soccer stars on the team. She was an orthopedic surgeon of all things, and the media had swooned over Liam falling for her. I hoped I didn't come across as a love struck idiot to her. Maybe lust struck was the better way to put it.

"Okay. I can handle finding her. Don't worry about me," I replied.

Ethan was quiet for a beat, his eyes searching mine—for what I didn't know. "Right then. I should be going."

He said that, but he didn't move. We stood there, pressed together with the air humming around us. He muttered something and then his lips crashed to mine. Inside of a millisecond, his tongue was tangling with mine. I'd come to learn any kiss with Ethan was hot, wet and over- powering. By the time he pulled away, I was flushed inside and out and on the verge of desperation. I didn't want him to leave. Not at all. Rather, I was wondering if we had time for him to sink inside of me.

He had far more control than I did and stepped away. The saving grace was the fierce need in his gaze. "Later," he said curtly before turning and striding quickly out of my office.

Chapter Fifteen

ETHAN

I caught the towel tossed my way and dragged it over my face. The sounds of the crowd were nothing but buzz to my ears. We'd barely squeaked out a win on this game, and I was bloody exhausted. The opposing team's offense had worked our defense to the bone. Alex, as usual, had managed to keep any shots out of the net, but that didn't mean we weren't fucking worn out. This same team had almost bested us last season too, and it felt like they were out for blood this year.

Someone nudged my shoulder, and I glanced up to see Liam. "Great work, mate. They made you boys work for it. The offense had it easy tonight," he said with a wink and a grin.

He handed over a bottle of water, which I promptly guzzled. I looked up toward the stands, my eyes landing on the owner's box where I knew Zoe was with Olivia. I loved knowing she was here. Back in London, I was accustomed to having my family watch me play. At any given game, one or all of my sisters were there, along with my parents. Ever since I'd signed with the Stars, it was rare for me to have anyone specifically here to see me play. My family had flown out a few times, but it wasn't the same. If I had to put my finger to one thing I missed playing here, it was that. As such, it felt strangely good to know Zoe was here. My heart tightened and gave a kick. I shied away from thinking too much about what that meant.

I'd been all but obsessed with Zoe ever since the other night with her. It was fair to say I'd *never* chased after a woman. But then it was fair to say no woman had even remotely affected me the way Zoe did. I didn't want to ponder about any of it. I just wanted to see her. Again and again and again.

With my teammates crowding around me, we made our way down the stadium hall toward the locker room. Alex nudged me and before I knew it, I was trapped in an after game interview with him. Since our defense had been all that stood between our team and a loss, we had to talk about it. Our offense had scored one goal, but otherwise, the opposing team had managed to control the game.

I still didn't understand the sports media in America. They wanted to talk to you right away when you couldn't even catch your fucking breath. For big games, they liked to do that *and* throw clusters of players up for longer questioning sessions after we showered. All in all, for a country that didn't have the fervor for true football the way the rest of the world did, it was rather confusing and tried my patience.

I managed to avoid the second round of interviews, but I was annoyed and worried Zoe might take off before I got to see her. I rushed through a shower and threw on clothes before heading out. The stadium hallway echoed with the murmur of voices from various points. As I rounded the corner to where Coach's office was, I smiled because I heard Zoe's voice. I leaned against the doorway to find Olivia with Bentley's leash curled in her hand talking with Zoe who was squatting down to pet Bentley. Bentley was Olivia and Liam's spoiled rotten dog. He was small and brown all over with one ear that stuck up. He was so endearing that basically anyone walking by slathered him with affection.

Zoe and Olivia didn't notice I was there, so I took the moment to enjoy the sight of Zoe. She'd changed since I saw her at work earlier. Aside from being bare naked with her, this was the first time I'd seen her in something other than her usual work uniform of a fitted skirt and blouse with a cropped jacket. By the way, I fucking loved those outfits. She looked so tidy and buttoned up, it made me want to just rip her clothes off. Yet, it was nice to see her more relaxed. She wore another skirt, this one of soft black fabric that twirled around her knees. It made me want to flip it up. She'd paired it with a pair of black cowboy boots and a silky white blouse. Fuck me. I was bloody exhausted, and my body started humming just at the sight of her.

Someone clapped me on the shoulder, and I glanced over to find Liam. I'd been so zoned out staring at Zoe I didn't even hear him approach me. He leaned against the opposite side of the door and winked at me. "So? Zoe," he said, his voice low.

Liam might've fallen head over heels in love with Olivia, but that hadn't cured him of his tendency to tease. Just now, he had a sly grin, and I knew he was hoping to get under my skin. Funny thing was, I didn't really care.

"That's right."

His grin faded, his gaze flicking to Olivia, Zoe and then back to me. "She's not your usual type."

Now *that* got to me. "Why...?" I started to ask, but then Olivia looked over.

"Hey boys!" she called as she dropped Bentley's leash and strode across Coach's office to Liam.

He promptly lifted her against him and kissed the hell out of her. Precisely what I wanted to do to Zoe. But that's not where things were with us. Perhaps if we'd been alone, I might've. Hell, I definitely would've done far more than that. It wasn't that I had a problem with heavy PDA. In fact, I was easy come, easy go with that. But then, all I'd ever done was casual. Zoe didn't feel casual, and I had no idea how she'd feel if I snogged her right here with Liam and Olivia as our audience and whoever else might walk by.

She straightened and looked over. The second her eyes locked with mine, it was as if a match lit the air between us, a flame licking its way across the room. Her hair was down. One look at those tousled auburn locks tumbling around her shoulders, and blood shot straight to my groin.

"You two out for a staring match?" Liam asked, his voice breaking into my fuzzed thoughts.

I glanced his way to find Olivia nudging him in the side with her elbow. She looked to Zoe. "Don't mind him. He doesn't know how to behave in public."

Zoe bit her lip and smiled. "Okay then." She straightened her shoulders and strolled over to us, stopping just in front of me. "Nice to see you again, Liam." Her eyes bounced between us. "Great game."

"Your boy here did most of the hard work," Liam added with a grin. "I had it easy tonight."

"We always do the hard work," I countered.

"Not always, mate, but tonight for certain," Liam returned with a roll of his eyes.

Though the air around us felt electric with Zoe near me, I sensed a reserve from her. Only belatedly did I realize she was likely worried about any appearance of impropriety. Little did she know that only made me want her more.

I relied on habit to get through a few more minutes of teasing from Liam and casual chatting with Olivia. I was relieved when Olivia nudged Liam and said they had to go. Though I wanted to slam Coach's office door shut and bend Zoe over the desk, I hedged my bets. I'd have better luck somewhere private. We walked alongside Liam and Olivia through the stadium hallway outside. With the crowd still filtering out, it wasn't likely anyone would notice Zoe with me. Knowing she'd likely be furious if I did what I wanted—

yank her to me and kiss her senseless without giving a bloody damn for anyone who noticed—I kept my hands to myself and played calm.

Meanwhile, lust surged through me. I'd meant what I'd said earlier that I wanted her to wear her hair down more, but I hadn't pondered the effect it would have on me. Between that and her flirty skirt, I was exercising phenomenal restraint. It was a damn good thing I was exhausted from the game, otherwise my tether would have snapped.

———

A bit later, I stood outside the entrance to Zoe's flat. I'd persuaded her to share a cab with me. Seeing as my flat was only a few blocks away, I'd hopped out and paid the cab driver before she could argue the point. I could tell she wanted to argue, so when she opened her mouth, I kissed her instead. That had flustered her enough, she'd shot me a glare but stayed quiet when I got out with her.

It wasn't rainy tonight, but the air was damp and cool. Her hair glinted from the streetlight nearby. She paused at the entrance, her hand curled on the handle as if she was holding on for dear life. When she looked over at me, she was chewing the inside of her cheek, and I could tell she was worrying about something.

"No need to worry, luv," I said without thinking.

Her eyes flashed and she cocked her head to the side. "What makes you think I'm worrying?"

I swear, she just wanted to be contrary with me. Fine. I stepped closer and reached over to slide my fingers through the ends of her hair, which conveniently happened to be over her breast. I could feel her nipple tighten against the backs of my fingers and took my time toying with her hair just to prolong the moment.

"Because you're doing that thing with your mouth," I explained.

Her eyes narrowed as she stared at me, but I didn't miss the flutter of her pulse in her neck and the way her breath came in short little pants. She was silent, long enough that the moment tightened around us and the air became heavy. I was coming to learn it was nigh impossible for me to be near her and not want her like mad. I was already hard, and we were just standing there.

"Invite me in," I said, my voice a gruff whisper.

I slid my fingers through her hair once more before lifting my hand and trailing a fingertip along her jaw and down the side of her neck. Her gaze held mine for an electric moment before she tore her eyes free and yanked her keys out of her purse. Inside of a hot minute, my hand was curled around hers as we made our way down the hallway upstairs, our footsteps echoing on the hardwood floor. The second the door to her flat clicked shut behind us, I spun her around and fit my mouth over hers.

She opened to me instantly, her tongue tangling with mine on a low moan. I pressed her back into the door and plastered myself to her. I needed—hell I needed more than I could even contemplate, but right now I needed to anchor myself against her. Every curve of her pressed to me, and the wild need drumming inside of me found a release valve.

I lost track of everything but the feel of her against me and the damp heat between her thighs against my throbbing cock. I wasn't much for rushing when it came to sex. I preferred to take my time and enjoy the ride, so to speak. It was fair to say I'd never lost control this way. Zoe made me bloody crazy. All thought went offline, and I was driven by nothing by hungry need and sensation.

I tore my lips free from hers only because I was frantic for the taste of her skin. I yanked at her blouse, barely registering that I tore the thin silk when a button tried to hold its ground against my tugging. We stumbled away from the door as she shoved my shirt up, swearing when it caught on my chin. I reached behind my neck to lift it free, sending it sailing to the floor. She was already busy unbuttoning my jeans and sliding her palm inside my briefs to free my cock.

I opened my eyes to see her breasts spilling out of the ridiculous excuse for a bra she was wearing—see through sheer black silk—and her nipples taut and pink and begging for me to suck them. I was distracted at the fact she was still in her skirt and boots and knew just what I wanted. I grabbed her hips and spun her around.

I hadn't meant to make her stumble, but it worked for me when she caught her balance on the wall. I flipped her skirt up over her bottom, just like I'd wanted to do ever since I'd laid eyes on her tonight. Fuck me. Her lush, generous bottom was bare to me with nothing but a slender strip of black silk tucked between her cheeks. As I steadied her with one hand on her hip, I slid my palm down her back, savoring the hitch in her breath as her spine arched. As if she read my mind, she flattened her other palm against the wall. With her skirt riding up over her hips and her boots on, I almost came just looking at her.

I slid my hand down between her cheeks, my breath hissing when I felt the wet silk between her thighs. I nudged them apart with a knee and shoved the silk out of the way, burying a finger knuckle deep inside of her. She pressed back into my touch and—another first for me—I was torn between how fucking sexy it would be to finger fuck her until she came, or sink inside of her soaking wet channel post haste. I drew my finger out and added another, stretching and teasing her channel until she was moaning and riding my hand. I meant to hold out, but yet again, it turned out my discipline was bloody weak when it came to her.

Still letting her ride the stroke of my fingers, I freed her hip and fumbled in my pocket, yanking my wallet out and using my teeth to free the condom tucked in it. I threw my wallet aside and smoothed the condom on in record time. I reluctantly eased my fingers out of her channel and glanced down. She was the sexiest woman I'd ever seen. No question about it. With her legs that went on forever, her sweet ass, her fiery hair and her pink, wet pussy, I'd have died happy if this sight was the last I ever saw. I must've waited a beat too long because she glanced over her shoulder and my knees buckled. Her lips were pink and swollen and her cheeks flushed. She arched back, pressing her drenched folds against my cock. The look in her eyes almost made me come.

I gripped my cock and positioned it at her entrance, the kiss of wet heat so tempting, it took every ounce of control I had to hold still for a beat. "Tell me what you want."

She pressed her hips into my cock, her eyes narrowing, and muttered something I couldn't hear.

"What, luv?"

"You. I want you!"

"You'll need to be more specific."

She tossed her hair back as she looked over her shoulder. "Shut up and fuck me."

How could I fail to follow an order like that? I surged into her creamy clench, straight to the hilt. Her head fell forward before she lifted it again when I began to move. She was so fucking wet and so fucking tight, I didn't know how long I'd last. Her entire channel pulsed and clenched around my cock. I forced myself to slow my strokes, savoring every inch of her throbbing around me. I gripped her hips and watched as she tilted her ass up and rode my cock like she'd been born to it.

The need to let go was roaring through me, but I held back, reaching around and swirling my thumb over her clit— a hot, wet little button. She cried my name between gasps, and I finally let go, my release hitting me like a shockwave. I had to catch my balance with a palm slapping against the wall. Our breath came in heaves and we stayed still like that —my cock buried deep inside of her—for several long moments.

She finally lifted her head and glanced over her shoulder at me. One look in her eyes—that dark swirl of gold and green—and my cock twitched. It should've been enough I'd just spent myself completely inside of her. But it wasn't. I was becoming uncomfortably aware that I might never get enough of her. The air felt weighted with a shimmering intimacy.

I didn't know what the hell to say. I usually had no trouble spouting off something suave, but I couldn't form a word. I simply stared at her. With one hand resting on her hips, I felt her skin prickling underneath and realized she was cold. That was enough to nudge me out of my passion-induced stupor.

I eased out of her and helped her straighten up. I didn't like moving away from her, not one bit. Next thing I knew, I was instructing her to kick off her boots, tugging her clothes off, lifting her into my arms and carting her into the shower. Another first. For all my tendencies as a player and one who had plenty of sex, I kept a clear boundary around certain matters. I didn't sleep in women's beds, and I certainly didn't shower with women. Those activities smacked of an intimacy I'd never sought. Yet, with Zoe, I didn't even consider my usual boundaries. In fact, I'd have been wrestling with disappointment if she tried to draw any lines.

We showered, and I almost fucked her again at the sight of soap bubbles on her skin and water running everywhere. The only thing that held me back was my belated recollection that this was only the second time she'd had actual sex. I was the opposite of an expert in this area, but I figured maybe I shouldn't overdo it.

After we toweled off and tossed on some clothes, I found myself leaning back into the cushions on her couch with her legs draped over mine. Her skin was rosy from our shower, and she looked delectably cute in a pair of swingy cotton sweatpants and a loose t-shirt. As I was pondering that I'd barreled my way into this, my stomach growled. Loudly.

Zoe arched a brow. "Hungry?"

My stomach gave its audible answer, and she grinned. "I didn't even think about the fact you're probably starving after a game like that."

"I'm always starving after I play. Doesn't matter how hard," I offered with a shrug.

She swung her legs off my lap and moved to get up. "I'll make..."

I caught her hand. "Don't."

She looked back at me. "Don't what?"

"Walk away. I'm too tired to follow you."

I was. The physical exhaustion I'd staved off on the fumes of my desire for her was hitting me broadside now.

"You need to eat," she countered.

"Order pizza. I'll pay," I said, pointing to my wallet still on the floor where I'd tossed it by the door earlier.

With a funny smile, she sank back down onto the couch and did as I asked. The only time she left my side was to answer the door for the pizza delivery. The last thing I remembered was finally not feeling hungry. Then, I came to at the feel of a blanket being draped over me. That galvanized me. Groggy and so fucking tired I could hardly move, I lurched up and muttered I didn't want to sleep alone. Moments later, I sighed into her hair against the pillows in her bed and pulled her soft form up against my side.

Chapter Sixteen

ZOE

I vaguely listened at a court hearing a few days later—a few days during which Ethan texted roughly every hour. I was able to surmise his daily practice schedule solely based on that being the longest chunk of time during the day he didn't text me. My mind wandered to what it had felt like to have him deep inside me, the pull and slide of his cock feeling so delicious I got hot and bothered just thinking about it.

"Ms. Lawson," the judge said.

My attention snapped back to the courtroom. I was relieved at the distance between the table where I was standing and the judge, otherwise he might notice the flush I could feel on my cheeks. "Yes, Your Honor."

"I've asked you twice if you agree to the conditions proposed by opposing counsel. This will be your last chance."

Judge Wilson was a generally patient judge, but I could see the furrow between his brows and sensed I needed to do a better job of focusing. This had never happened to me before. I didn't get distracted in court, even for the mundane administrative hearings such as this one. I'd always prided myself on my focus and attention to detail. Little did I know, I'd been coasting by on the fact I had nothing to distract me before. Ethan was the mother of all distractions and filled my mind day and night.

"My apologies Your Honor. I've reviewed the conditions in the proposed settlement and my client is willing to agree to them," I replied with a nod.

The moment the judge turned back to opposing counsel to ask something, Ethan sauntered right back into my thoughts. I was screwed. In more ways than one.

I got through the hearing and made my way back outside. As much as my mind was enjoying fantasies of Ethan, worries were cropping up. I'd obliterated the professional barrier I tried to keep between myself and clients. When it came to attorneys and clients, the ethical guidelines around relationships were vague. The general line was whether the 'sexual contact' started before your professional relationship. I was walking right on that line, and I knew it. Ethan had kissed me before I became his attorney, but I felt silly arguing that point. No matter the legal ramifications of what I'd done, it was definitely frowned upon to fuck your clients. As with everything in life, men could get away with far more than women. I knew how it would look if it became public knowledge I'd gotten involved with Ethan while I was representing him.

I hated admitting it, but he'd swept me off my feet and I'd gotten caught in the tides of desire. I'd conveniently managed to shut my worries off for a bit, but now they were back in force. In part because I didn't know how to define what was happening with us. I knew, whether I wanted to or not, that he was best known for being a player and not just in soccer. I doubted he intended to have this thing with me be anything more than it was. I figured the heat would start to cool, and he'd move onto the next hot woman who caught his fancy.

So I needed to stop being stupid and think clearly. The

last thing I wanted was to tarnish the professional reputation I'd cultivated so carefully. The smart move would be to put the brakes on what was happening with Ethan. I'd managed to wave goodbye to my annoying virginity, so I could probably have more luck with a normal dating life as a twenty-nine year old woman now. Problem was, just thinking about trying to be with anyone other than Ethan made my heart ache.

This was bad. Really, really bad. I could *not* fall for him.

Why not? He's totally into you. You're not just another woman to him.

Yeah, right. Don't be so stupid. I'm a novelty right now. It will wear off and then where will I be if I let myself think we can have something more?

This internal debate was replaying like an intense match day in and day out. I needed to get a grip and fast. As I strode quickly down the sidewalk to return to my office, my phone vibrated in my pocket. I slipped it out to see Ethan's name flash on a text banner. A smile bloomed from the inside out. I tapped it open.

Please.

He was back at inviting me to every meal of the day. Meanwhile, I'd been staving him off by telling him I was busy.

I couldn't help myself.

Fine. Dinner tonight.

Yes! Okay, meet you at your place at 5:30.

My heart did a little dance and my belly somersaulted. I was screwed, so totally screwed.

———

I took a gulp of wine as Liam regaled the table with an amusing story about him and Alex when they were boys. We were at a large round table in the back corner of a newer Italian restaurant on the Seattle scene. Seattle was a foodie city. Restaurants churned through here, some surviving the onslaught of attention and others slinking away. I didn't even recall what this place was called, but the food was divine. The menu hewed to fairly classic Italian dishes with fresh ingredients.

Ethan had arrived promptly at five-thirty to pick me up as he'd promised. I'd come to learn he was a punctual man. His outer image as a lackadaisical player didn't mesh with much of what I'd come to know about him. He was unfailingly polite, although he never missed an opportunity to tease. Tonight was more eye opening than I could've imagined. Dinner included Liam and Olivia, Tristan who was Ethan's flat-mate and another player for the Stars, along with Harper Jacobs who I'd met when I was representing Alex Gordon last year, and Daisy Knight who was a good friend of Olivia and Harper's. Alex wasn't here, which had surprised me until Harper shared he was out of town for the weekend.

It felt strange to be here with Ethan. For starters, there was the obvious fact I hadn't had anything resembling a relationship since I'd been in law school and even then, nothing had gone far. Aside from Olivia and Liam, Ethan and I were the only other two who could be considered a couple. Despite my renewed worries about what the hell I was doing to my career by doing anything with Ethan, I hadn't even thought about being seen in public with him until we were here. When I wasn't caught up in conversation, I was busy trying to convince myself if anyone saw me here, I could easily explain it since I was with an entire group, most of whom weren't on dates. Truth was, I didn't really want to think about it, what with Ethan alternating between keeping his hand curled over my thigh, or sliding it in between my legs. The end result was I was hot, bothered, flustered and drinking too much wine.

"Mate, Alex tells a different story," Ethan said with a sly grin. "According to him, you're the one who fell in the lake."

Liam flashed a grin. He didn't give me the crazy zing

Ethan did, but I had to admit Liam was ridiculously hand-some with his jet black hair and blue eyes. It was beyond obvious he adored Olivia, so I imagined he'd left many a broken heart in his wake. "Aye, Alex isn't here to debate that point," Liam countered.

Tristan, a quiet sort, winked toward Ethan. "My bets are on Alex, mate. He's more methodical than you."

I'd lost track of Liam's story, but I knew it involved one of them falling in a lake. Conversation moved in another direction. I didn't mind groups like this, but I tended to be a quiet participant. My ears perked up when someone mentioned Ethan's sisters.

"You have sisters?" I asked, glancing his way. I didn't ponder my intense curiosity, but it was there. I wanted to *know* him and was hungry for every little personal detail I discovered.

"Oh luv, he has four," Liam interjected, answering for him. "For that reason, I always turn to him when I need a female perspective. All through university, he was our go to for advice. He'd call up one of his sisters and hand the phone over."

Ethan chuckled and shrugged. "Forgot about that. Loads of questions back then about how not to chase girls."

"Four sisters?" Daisy said, brushing her long blonde hair back from her shoulders. She reminded me of Jana in ways. She was bold and beautiful with her bright blonde hair and wide brown eyes. She didn't shy away from any topic. I'd also noticed her attention flicking to Tristan with frequency. He took tall, dark and mysterious to a new level. If he noticed her attention, it didn't show. Back to the question at hand.

"That's correct. Four whole sisters. Three older and one younger, and every one of them bosses me around," Ethan answered with a grin.

Liam caught my eyes. "Zoe, if you have trouble with Ethan, just sic one of his sisters on him. They'll whip him into shape inside of one phone call."

Ethan gave my thigh a squeeze while he laughed at Liam's comment. "True. I tend to do what they say."

Daisy flashed a grin. "You're smarter than you let on, Ethan."

The banter continued, and I drank another glass of wine. I didn't realize quite how tipsy I was until we were leaving, and I began walking out of the restaurant. I wobbled a bit, and Ethan caught me around the waist. I was relieved everyone there with us was ahead of us because I didn't like to think about how this looked. I leaned into him because I was like a cat looking for affection when it came to Ethan. I leaned into every touch, my body thrumming.

"Easy luv. I think you might've had a few too many glasses of wine," he murmured, his voice near my ear and his breath gusting against my neck.

A shiver ran through me. I glanced up to him. "Too much is one way to put it," I managed. "Did you have anything to drink?"

He shook his head, his mouth curling in one of those dangerous grins and his green eyes glinting in the dim light. "No. My attorney told me I had to behave."

This should've bothered me. Instead, I wanted to kiss him. God, a man shouldn't be allowed to have a mouth like his. He had generous, mobile lips. I knew how they felt on mine, and I wanted them there. Now. Instead, I stumbled slightly again.

Ethan gathered me against his side and somehow maneuvered us through the door. Everyone but Liam and Olivia was gone. They were waiting just outside the restaurant. Liam was lifting her palm and dropping a kiss in the center of it, his eyes locked to hers. For a beat, I felt lonely. I wanted someone to look at me like that. The moment snapped when Olivia looked our way. With her porcelain skin, dark curls and green eyes, she was lovely, just lovely. I liked her and could imagine being friends with her. She was brilliant and also focused on her career as an orthopedic surgeon. I wanted to ask her how it was to fit a man like Liam into her life and make it work. That would have to be a conversation for another time though.

"Zoe, I'm glad you came tonight. We do this almost every weekend, so please join us anytime," Olivia said with a warm smile as Ethan essentially dragged me to them.

If she noticed how tipsy I was, she didn't let on. "I shall invite her for next week," Ethan said.

Olivia glanced between us before narrowing her gaze at him. "Zoe might be too good for you. You'd better treat her well."

My heart gave a hard thump at that. Ethan tightened his arm around my waist, and I sensed a thread of defensiveness in him. "I'd never do anything otherwise."

Liam said something just before a cab rolled up. They said their goodbyes, and then I was standing on the sidewalk with Ethan, fuzzily wondering what to do. I needn't have wondered. He hailed a cab and bundled me into it. Before I knew it, he was walking beside me in the hallway to my apartment and scooping up the keys I dropped on the floor. Once we were inside, I tackled him. All I wanted was to kiss him. His tongue slid against mine before he drew back quickly.

"Bed for you," he announced.

That wouldn't do. I wanted him. All of him.

"No. I want..."

I leaned toward him to kiss him again, but miscalculated with my lips landing on his jaw.

He caught me and turned me around. "Trust me luv, I want you. Badly. But you're drunk, and I don't do drunk."

I was too drunk to argue much, so I allowed him to drag me to my bedroom and help me out of my clothes. His eyes grew dark, and I could see the ridge of his cock behind the jeans that hugged him like a lover. My knees gave out and I plunked on the bed in nothing but a scrap of silk thong.

Next thing I knew he was pulling his t-shirt off and dragging it over my head.

"Ooh, this smells like you," I announced.

I grabbed for him. "When did you become so uptight?" I muttered. "I bet you've had plenty of drunk sex." I reached out and roughly dragged my hand over his cock, grinning when his breath hissed out.

He'd been in the midst of kicking off his shoes. His gorgeous green gaze swept over me. "I don't do drunk with you."

I reached up to stroke his cock again, but he grabbed my hand.

I glared at him. "Why?"

He gave his head a little shake, something flickering in his gaze. "Because," he said firmly.

He felt oddly protective. I didn't know what to make of that, and I felt funny inside. In short order, he tucked me in bed and climbed in beside me. He removed his jeans, so I could feel the heat of his cock against my hip.

I meant to say something, to argue my point—whatever my point was—but I fell asleep.

Hours later, I woke in the darkness, momentarily disoriented. I wasn't used to having anyone sleep with me, so it was strange to awaken and feel a presence beside me. After a beat, I remembered it was Ethan. I could've really gotten used to sleeping with him. I tended to get chilled at night, but not with him beside me. He was so warm, my own personal furnace. I apparently liked to drape myself all over him. I had one leg thrown over his with my foot hooked between his calves and was lying half atop his chest. And what a chest it was. Even relaxed in sleep, every inch of him was hard, honed muscle.

I breathed in his scent and sighed. His arm was curled around me. His palm slid up my hip in a sleepy caress, and I burrowed closer because it felt so good.

"Mmm...Zoe?"

"Uh huh."

"You awake?" he asked, his voice gravelly from sleep.

I laughed against his chest. "Uh huh."

"Go back to sleep," he murmured with another sleepy caress up my side.

My heart squeezed and emotion rocked me. His hand stilled after another pass and his breathing evened out. I fell asleep with him warm and strong beside me.

Chapter Seventeen

ETHAN

I guzzled a bottle of water and stripped out of my clothes before striding quickly into the showers. We'd had a long practice today. Management had signed two new players, so Coach was working us harder than usual to help them mesh. Coach Bernie was all about team stuff. Being in the starting line up offered no privileges on his team. Hell, I was bloody certain nothing would get Coach to treat any player special. Occasionally, I grumbled for the sake of it, but I actually liked it. I'd been playing football since I was a boy in Britain. I'd played on many amalgamations of teams. The higher the level of competition, the more prima donnas you encountered. There'd been a few idiots on my team in university. I'd lucked into the same team with Liam and Alex once we started playing professionally in London. Back there, we had a great team, but the coach let some problem players slide as long as they pulled their shit together when we had games.

Alex had been the backup goalkeeper for a bit until the bloody arse who used to be the starting goalkeeper finally pushed the limits too far with his partying and showing up hung over. Most of my mates, myself included, had been beyond pissed at how long that shit dragged out. My point was I didn't mind Coach making us run extra for the sake of team spirit even if I bitched about it sometimes. I rested my palms on the cool tile wall and let the hot water pound over me. The shower echoed with occasional talking as we all washed away a few hours of sweat and grit.

After I was showered and dressed and heading down the echoing hallway, I paused when I heard my name just after passing by Coach's office. I took a few steps back and glanced in. At his wave, I stepped inside.

"Should I close the door?" I asked.

Coach nodded. "Please do."

Coach often snagged us for little chats, so I didn't think much of it. I figured he wanted to ask me about the new players. I closed the door behind him and sat down across from him, promptly catching the mini basketball he'd just tossed toward a hoop in the wall. It hit the rim and bounced right to me. He grinned when I tossed it back to him.

Another throw and the ball swished through the hoop. Coach let it roll across the floor and faced me. He ran a hand through his typically mussed gray hair and eyed me for a beat, his blue gaze considering.

"Rumor has it you're dating Zoe Lawson," he said calmly.

My mouth fell open and then I snapped it shut. My mind started running through various machinations. If I weren't worried about what Zoe might prefer me to say, I'd simply state the truth.

Coach chuckled and rested his chin in his hand. "Ah, I see then."

"You see what?" I managed, hoping my usual manners would stave off any giveaway about what I might be thinking.

"The look on your face tells me yes," he added.

Fuck. If Zoe wanted to keep things between us on the lowdown, I'd obviously blown it. I'd conveniently blocked out her initial worry about having anything to do with me.

Hell, I'd blocked out all kinds of things when it came to her, including the disconcerting effect she had on me—namely, she'd pretty much taken up residence in my brain and body. I was beginning to suspect she might be on her way to stealing more than that, but I wasn't quite ready to go there yet.

I opened and closed my mouth, like a bloody fish, while I tried to sort out what to say to Coach.

He sighed and leaned back in his chair. "Ethan, I don't care if you're dating Ms. Lawson. I have to say, she doesn't strike me as your type, but I think that might mean you're maturing. The only thing I care about is making sure you resolve those silly charges. If you *are* involved with Ms. Lawson, I'm thinking it might be best if we speak with her about alternative representation for you."

I was shaking my head before he finished. He arched a brow.

"You have a problem with that? From everything Ms. Lawson has shared with me, it's a matter of formalities at this point. You were certainly in the wrong place at the wrong time and intoxicated enough to get yourself in a fix, but I don't think this warrants a problem with changing attorneys."

My heart was pounding—hard enough it startled me— and my head was spinning. The thing was, I trusted Zoe completely. I didn't want anyone else to handle anything to do with my stupid legal situation. It had to be her and only her. I stared over at Coach, my head shaking on its own again.

Coach was quiet before he shook his head in return. "Look, obviously you can make your own decision on this. I suggested this more for Ms. Lawson's sake than yours."

"Pardon?"

Coach's perceptive gaze held mine for a few beats, and I got uncomfortable. Sometimes he was crazy smart about people, well most of the time as far as I could tell. I couldn't say I enjoyed feeling like he was sussing me out.

"I'm guessing Ms. Lawson might not appreciate the attention that comes with being involved with you. Particularly if she's representing you. If the situation for your charges wasn't simple, I'd be insisting."

I knew his point to be true. In the years I'd been in the public spotlight, I largely ignored the media attention. In fact, I found it mostly a source of amusement. The nicknames and the silliness of it all weren't worth letting myself get bothered. Yet, I'd never had to worry about its effect on someone close to me. I'd watched Liam and Alex navigate this tricky field when they moved into the territory of serious relationships, as determined by the gossip media. It was fair to say I'd never even come close to a serious relationship, much less had any woman in my orbit who might care if they came under public scrutiny.

I didn't know how to define what was happening with Zoe. However, I knew beyond even a thread of doubt she would *not* want to deal with the glare of the media attention that might come if it became known we were involved. Every time I tried to wrap my brain around what she meant to me, it was like static. The sound of the basketball swishing through the hoop again cued me that I'd zoned out.

I looked back over at Coach. Because he was a decent man, he'd let me be to spin the wheels uselessly in my brain. He glanced my way and arched a brow.

"I'll talk to her," I finally said.

He tossed the ball once again and spun to face me. "You do that." He paused as if considering his words. "You seem a little off about the whole thing. If I were a betting man, I'd say Ms. Lawson might mean more to you than you considered. Don't let that scare you off."

That static started up in my brain again. After a beat, I gave my head a shake. Unsure what to say, I fell back on something vague. "I'll think about that."

Coach didn't grin, but a gleam entered his eyes. "Fair enough. Let me know tomorrow after you speak with her."

I managed to politely excuse myself from his office and headed to my flat. I had to hold back from the urge to turn down the side street that led to Zoe's flat. I walked into the flat I shared with Tristan, wondering if he happened to be around. I was in luck. He was standing in front of the refrigerator, staring inside.

"Hey mate," he called over his shoulder as he let the refrigerator door fall closed and turned to face me. He took a few steps and hooked his foot on a stool by the counter as he sat down.

"I'm probably calling out for pizza. Want some?" he asked

"Perfect. I forgot our grocery run this week."

Tristan arched a brow and grinned. "I noticed. You've forgotten a lot the last few weeks."

Before I had a chance to argue the point, he was tapping his phone screen and ordering pizza. I kicked off my shoes and threw myself down on the couch. After he hung up, Tristan meandered over and joined me, handing me a bottle of water when he sat down.

He knew I tended to guzzle several after practice. I made quick work of the water and then set the bottle on the coffee table before eyeing him. "What the hell do you mean I've forgotten a lot the last few weeks?"

Tristan met my gaze steadily. "Exactly that. If you ask me, Zoe's got you tied up in knots. Not a bad thing though."

My heart gave a funny little kick as I stared back at him. "I'm not tied up in knots. I'm just..."

My words ran out because I didn't know what to say next. I didn't want to admit it, but he'd zeroed in on precisely what was bothering me. I'd never in my life worried about a woman and what she meant to me. I was the king of casual hook ups. I wasn't an arse, not like so many other guys, who treated women like crap and used them. But I definitely toed the line of lighthearted and casual. I made that perfectly clear and backed off fast if I sensed someone wanted more than that from me.

This thing with Zoe had snuck up on me. It had started simply enough—she was fucking gorgeous and all uptight and I just wanted to rattle her. Back when I'd first met her briefly when she was dealing with Alex's mess, I hadn't thought much beyond the fact I wanted her. She'd represented a challenge, one I wanted to win. Yet, back then, my interactions with her had been so brief and transitory, I hadn't had much chance to think beyond that. I couldn't have known getting close to her would send me into a tailspin like this.

Tristan cut into my rambling train of thought. "Stop thinking about it so much. You obviously like her. Why not just enjoy it?"

I eyed him and shrugged, internally restless and irritated. "You're one to give me romance advice," I said with a roll of my eyes.

He returned my shrug. "Hey mate, it's not my thing. I prefer my sanity. Sex is just that. No need to worry about anything more. I can see Zoe's getting to you because I'm not you. Objectivity is impossible in your own head."

My irritation faded because I knew I was more annoyed with my situation than with Tristan. "Of course. Maybe I do like her, but it doesn't mean I'm tied in knots."

He flashed a grin, standing the moment our door buzzer sounded. "Whatever you say, mate."

I elected to let the topic drop. Tristan's accuracy was too close for comfort at the moment. We inhaled our pizza and then he pulled out his laptop and buried his nose in studying.

I toyed with staying home for the night, but I was restless to go ahead and talk to Zoe, so I texted her and headed to her office.

Chapter Eighteen

ZOE

"Let me check my calendar," I said, turning to glance at my computer.

I was just finishing up a meeting with another attorney, Mark Smithson. He'd asked me for consultation and representation in a domestic dispute case with his ex. Mark was a high-profile corporate lawyer in Seattle. He likely made more money in a week than I did all year. I'd been surprised when he called. I hadn't agreed to take the case yet and would be reviewing the legal documents before I made a decision.

"How about next Wednesday at ten?" I asked, glancing back at him.

Mark was the epitome of suave. He wore black suits that probably cost a small fortune. He had straight dark hair and dark eyes. I could objectively notice he was handsome, but he didn't do a thing for me. He was too polished and carried himself as if he expected women to notice him. He'd been all compliments when he arrived today, declaring he'd heard great things about my work. I appreciated that, but it was also pointless. I had a thread of unease about him, and I couldn't put my finger on why.

Mark glanced at his phone and tapped the screen a few times. "I'll make it work," he replied with a smile.

I surmised the smile was intended to make me feel special. He had a way of maintaining eye contact that felt too purposeful. For a flash, it made me think of Ethan. He had an intense, direct way of looking at you. Yet, with Ethan, it didn't feel calculated. It was just how he was. He approached everything quite directly. I shook him out of my head and nodded at Mark before standing to walk him out.

As I opened my office door, I heard Ethan's voice—that distinct British accent of his with the teasing underlay. My belly fluttered and heat rolled through me, along with a little buzz of joy. I shouldn't have gotten so excited he was here, but *should* and *shouldn't* ideas only seemed to amp up everything I felt about Ethan. Distracted, I didn't notice Mark had stepped a little too close for comfort as we walked to the reception area.

Ethan glanced over just as Mark slid his hand around my waist and dropped a kiss on my cheek. I was so surprised, my body jerked away.

Mark, ever smooth and polished, merely smiled. "I'll hear from you soon. Thank you, Zoe."

The familiarity and warmth to his tone grated on me and confused me. I didn't know what he meant, but I didn't particularly like it. I was tempted right then and there to tell him I wouldn't take his case, but I forced myself to stay quiet. The last thing I needed was to piss off a lawyer who could send rumblings around about my work. I'd find a professional reason to turn his case down and calmly explain over the phone.

Ethan's eyes narrowed and his jaw tightened as he flicked his gaze from me to Mark. He stayed where he was by Jana's desk. Jana glanced our way as well, a flash of annoyance flickering in her eyes. She'd immediately informed me she thought Mark was an arrogant prick before she escorted him into my office for his appointment. I knew she'd notice his too close for comfort touch and get protective. Before anything else could happen, I stepped away from Mark to the desk.

Feigning a focus on the calendar on Jana's desk, I spoke over my shoulder. "Thank you, Mark. I'll take a look and let you know what I think," I managed to say.

He left the office. A few seconds passed after the outer door shut behind him before Jana spoke. "Oh my God. What the fuck was that about?" she demanded, rapidly flipping a pen back and forth between her fingers.

"I have no idea. He startled me," I muttered with a shrug.

Jana looked over at Ethan and then back to me. The air was tense, and I didn't quite know what to do about it.

"You're not taking his case, right?" Jana asked.

I shook my head fervently. "Definitely not. I just need to find a reason to say no that won't piss him off."

I finally looked back to Ethan. His eyes were dark and he was unusually still. A thread of unease slid through me. "Hey, I didn't know you were stopping by," I said, aiming for a light tone.

"I texted, but it looks like you were busy. Can we talk?" he said abruptly.

Before I had a chance to reply, Jana was standing up. "You two chat, but I'm taking off. I promised myself I wouldn't blow off my workout today." She grabbed her purse and jacket before all but running out the main door. "I'll lock up since it's after six," she said quickly as she whirled away.

The door bolt clicked audibly behind Jana. I was standing at the corner of her desk with Ethan a few feet away in front of it. He stared at me, a muscle in his jaw visibly clenching. The air felt heavy, taut with something I didn't quite recognize. It mingled with the usual hum between us. I couldn't seem to be anywhere near Ethan without my body feeling alive with need.

After a few beats, he spoke. "Who was that?"

"Mark Smithson. He's a big deal corporate lawyer who asked me to consider representing him in a domestic dispute. I've never met him until today. I won't be taking his case because... Well, he makes me uncomfortable. I just need to give him a decent reason for saying no. I can't really tell him I'm turning his case down because he makes me feel weird."

Ethan nodded tightly. After another heavy silence, he closed the distance between us. I could feel the heat and strength of him once he was directly in front of me. His eyes coasted over my face and dipped down. It was as if he was actually touching me. Everywhere his eyes landed, sparks skittered under the surface of my skin. After a moment, he lifted a hand and caught the ends of my hair in his fingers, idly twirling it.

I'd taken to wearing it down more often than I used to. I didn't quite want to admit to myself it was because Ethan asked me to, but that was the reason.

"I stand corrected," he said gruffly.

"About what?"

"It's not fair for me to say it, but I don't want you to wear your hair down. I'm not usually a selfish man, but when it comes to you it seems I am."

"Oh," was all I could manage. I should've thought it was ridiculous he cared who saw my hair down, but I didn't. Instead, thinking of it sent liquid need spinning through my veins.

His gaze darkened and he slid his fingers into my hair to cup the nape of my neck. A prickle of awareness ran down my spine. I opened my mouth to say something—nothing sensible—and then his mouth slammed against mine.

His kiss was hard, hot and overpowering. His tongue

tangled roughly with mine as he stepped closer, bumping me into the desk behind us. He tore his lips free and blazed a hot wet trail down the side of my neck, kissing, licking and nipping his way down into the valley between my breasts. Everything he did was rougher than usual, and I *loved* it. He yanked at my shirt, tearing the flimsy cotton at the corner of where it buttoned.

He paused for a beat, dragging his lips off of my skin and lifting his head. His eyes flicked to mine and then back down. My nipples were already so tight they ached. He loosened his hand from my hair and trailed his forefinger down my neck to circle one nipple and then the other. A fractured moan broke from me. I was already soaking wet, the silk between my thighs damp, and I wanted him inside of me. *Now.*

Though I might've been a virgin before Ethan, I wasn't completely inexperienced. I'd dated and made out often enough in college to know that, until Ethan, not one single man could work me up like he did. It had only been minutes since Jana locked the door behind her. Sex hadn't even been on my radar before that. Now, it wasn't enough for him to close his lips over a nipple, wetting the thin silk and driving me wild. My hips were rocking against him, restless for the hard heat of his cock to fill me.

"Ethan, don't..."

Whatever I meant to say got lost in a low keening moan when he sucked a nipple into his mouth and scored it lightly with his teeth. He drew back and lifted his head.

"Don't what, luv?"

I managed, with a bit of effort, to drag my eyes open. "Make me wait," I choked out when he arched into the cradle of my hips.

His eyes darkened further and he slid his hands down to the hem of my fitted skirt. In a flash, he'd yanked it up around my waist and was dragging my silk panties off. I kicked them free before he lifted me onto the desk. His eyes flicked down, and he dragged a finger through my folds. "I love how wet you get," he murmured, his voice

rough.

Much as everything he did only made me wilder inside, I was restless and needed him inside of me as soon as humanly possible. I reached between us and undid his fly inside of a second, sighing at the feel of his cock—hot and velvety— when I shoved his jeans and briefs down just enough so it bounced free. I started to yank him closer, but he pushed my hands away as he reached into his back pocket.

I shook my head and swatted at his hand. "I want to feel you," I murmured.

When he froze, his eyes locking to mine, I suddenly got self-conscious. I hadn't told him I'd been on the pill all this time. Jana had dragged me down to take care of that matter months ago. She'd declared she thought it was stupid not to be on the pill as a back up. She'd had her own pregnancy scare once upon a time, all over a broken condom, so she was practical about it. She'd been determined to make sure I didn't let the lack of birth control keep me forever a virgin. I'd also done some sleuthing on professional athletes and learned they were routinely screened. With that and the knowledge that Ethan was absolute when it came to his condom use, I figured it was safe to carry on without worrying about them. What made me want to squirm was it was all over wanting to feel him with nothing between us.

Ethan was quiet, his eyes boring into me. The air got heavier around us, weighted with a depth of emotion I didn't know how to interpret. My heart thudded against my ribs as I stared at him.

"I'm on the pill, and I just thought maybe it..."

I stopped talking when he shook his head sharply. "Obviously it's okay. If you were wondering, I'm clean. I get tested every few months. We all do."

"I figured," I muttered, getting more embarrassed by the minute. Somehow admitting what I wanted—no barriers between us—felt huge, and I didn't quite know what to do with it. "I'm clean too," I added, belatedly realizing that was probably pointless, seeing as I'd been a virgin before him and hadn't even gone on a date anytime in the recent past. Intellectually speaking, I knew there were other ways to worry, but I wasn't thinking too sensibly just then.

His mouth curled at one corner, and he finally dropped the hand that had been hooked in his back pocket. Only to lift it and brush my hair away from my face. Shivers chased in the wake of his touch when his fingers brushed my ear.

His eyes never left mine as he reached between us and positioned his cock at my entrance. He held still for a beat before sinking inside, his eyes falling closed on a rough groan.

I almost came right then. I was so emotionally wrought and already teetering on the edge. It didn't take much with him. It felt so amazing to feel him bare inside of me. I could feel every ridge of his hard cock. My body adjusted to him filling me. I didn't realize my eyes had fallen closed until he spoke.

"Zoe."

Through the haze of need, I met his gaze. I felt almost drunk—it felt that good to be with him like this.

He stared at me hard, his gaze searching—for what I didn't know. "I don't think I can take seeing another man touch you. I thought I was going to fucking lose my mind when he kissed you."

His words were fierce.

My answer was swift and true. "I barely know him. I didn't want him to touch me. I don't know why he did."

"I know," he murmured, his lips so close to mine, I could feel them move. "It wasn't you, but it doesn't change that it made me want to clock him."

I shouldn't have savored his words, but I did. It felt oddly good knowing he felt possessive of me. I meant to say something else, but he curled his hands around my hips and pulled me past the edge of the desk, looking down as he began to move.

My gaze followed his. I watched as he drew back and sank inside of me again and again. The sight of his cock, wet and glistening from my fluids, sliding in and out of my swollen folds nearly undid me. It was so hot.

Chapter Nineteen

ETHAN

I almost lost control the second I sank inside of Zoe. In all the years I'd run wild, enjoying plenty of casual sex, I'd never, ever had sex without a condom. If there was a religion dedicated to the rigors of protected sex, I worshipped at its altar. If I didn't want to be committed, I couldn't expect anything more from anyone I was with. So, at thirty, I was a bareback virgin. Bloody hell, I'd had no idea what I'd been missing.

I'd been hanging on to a thin thread of control ever since that fucking asshole, Mark whoever-the-hell-he-was, had been all smarmy and put his hand on her waist and fucking kissed her cheek. She might not have picked up on it, but I knew exactly what he'd been doing. I might not be an ass, but I knew one when I met one. He was like a dog pissing on a tree, trying to mark his territory. Zoe, for all of her brilliance and professional confidence, didn't quite pick up on the depth of his bullshit.

Zoe's core was hot, slick and wet. I gripped her hips and sank into her to the hilt—again and again and again. Her channel started to throb around me—fucking hell it felt good—and those little breathy moans she made were raining down around us. I felt when she was almost there and reached between us, stroking my thumb in a circle around her slippery wet and swollen clit. She cried out, my name a broken shout, and the walls of her core pulsed around my cock. I distantly heard her knock something over as she caught her balance with her hands on the desk. My own release thundered through me with such force it was a damn good thing I had her to hold onto.

I was certain it was the longest and hardest orgasm I'd ever had. When I'd spent myself in her, the haze in my mind cleared enough that I noticed my fingers were digging into her luscious hips. I eased my grip and curled my arms around her, pulling her close against me. I didn't quite know what to do with the emotion roaring through me, so I held her tight and breathed in the scent of her.

After a few minutes, with nothing but the sound of our breath in the quiet room, Zoe lifted her head from where she'd tucked it against my shoulder. I opened my eyes, and my heart gave a decisive thump. Her hazel gaze met mine. For a flash, I felt uncertain, but then I saw a similar uncertainty reflected in her gaze and the tension inside of me eased. I smoothed her hair back, idly counting the freckles dusting her nose.

She squeaked when the door handle to the outer door rattled. I couldn't help but grin. Her eyes whipped from me to the door and back again.

"Can they hear us?" she hissed.

"Maybe," I whispered back, unable to resist winding her up a bit.

As if the universe was trying to help me out, the doorknob rattled again and whoever was out there knocked a few times.

"Oh my God!" Zoe said as she started to shimmy away from me.

Considering that I'd recently discovered that being bare inside of her was truly the most spectacular feeling in the world, I wasn't having that. I slid my hands down her sides and held her in place.

"Don't think so, luv. The door's bolted, so no one's coming in. Ease up, okay?"

Her eyes flicked to mine, and the furrow between her brows smoothed slightly. "What if they can see us through the glass?"

I glanced over my shoulder. The reception area had a single door with frosted glass panes framing the door on either side. I looked back to her and shrugged, just as we heard the sound of footsteps moving away from the door.

"Much as I'd love to get you worked up over that, all anyone can see through that is blurry shapes."

She bit the inside of her cheek and sighed. I could feel the tension leaving her body now that the unknown visitor had walked away. "You make me do crazy things," she muttered.

My chest was tight, and my heart set to thudding against my ribs. She had no fucking clue the crazy effect she had on me, but I elected not to elaborate on that right now. I managed a breath and looked down at her. "Oh, don't go blaming this all on me, luv. You were just as impatient as me."

Her cheeks flushed cherry red, and she bit her lip. My cock, still buried inside of her, twitched again.

"I wasn't blaming it on you. It's just I can't believe where we are," she murmured.

The office phone rang, and she jumped a little. She glanced back to me. "Are you going to let me move anytime soon?"

Much as I didn't want her to move and had a firm grip on her hips, logically I knew we couldn't stay here all night. With a grin, I eased out of her. I helped her get her clothes back in place and tucked myself back into my briefs and jeans.

I didn't know what to do with the feeling coursing through me. The idea of walking out of here without being with Zoe for the rest of the night made me feel restless and uncomfortable. I might not quite know what to do with how I felt, but the only refuge from my confusion was Zoe herself.

I waited while she returned to her office and powered off her computer and put away some files. I couldn't help but savor the sight of her long legs as she strode from her desk to the filing cabinet in the corner. Fuck me. This woman had me by the balls, and I hadn't the slightest clue what to do about it.

The asshole who she'd been meeting with earlier filtered back into my thoughts when she brushed her hair off her shoulders. I'd never, ever in my life been jealous of another guy. I'd taken one look at him and the way he treated Zoe and wanted to pummel his face and then fuck the hell out of her. I supposed I should count myself lucky I hadn't taken it upon myself to punch his cocky face. I could only imagine the headlines that would've gone with that.

This train of thought looped me back to what had prompted me to come see her this evening. I was supposed to talk to her about the whole representation thing. I knew it would bother her, and I didn't want to worry her. Yet, I'd promised Coach.

She locked the filing cabinet and then tugged her jacket on, glancing to me expectantly when she reached me where I was leaning inside the door. "You didn't have to wait for me," she said softly.

"I'm walking you home."

We hadn't openly discussed what I'd determined would happen. I'd walk her home and spend the night because I was coming to learn sleeping with Zoe was far, far better than sleeping alone. That's what I told myself. It was true, so

I could avoid the undercurrent of emotion rushing inside. The intimacy I felt with Zoe was starting to feel like the air I needed to breathe. It made me want to shy away, but I needed it. Needed her. More than I'd ever needed anything in my life.

"Oh. Are you sure? I mean, I don't want you to think..."

I reached for her hand, reeled her to me, and kissed her. I forced myself to keep it brief. Not an easy task, given that her lips were sublime. "I want to walk you home."

At that moment, her stomach growled. She clapped her hand over it. "Gah!"

"How about we order takeout? Don't try to tell me you're not hungry."

She grinned. "I won't. Are you sure you don't have other plans? I can certainly feed myself."

Bloody hell. Why did she have to be so damned independent? She kept making me say aloud the things that made me uncomfortable inside.

"I don't have any other plans, and I'm starving," I countered.

All of it was true. I might've eaten right before I came here, but losing my mind with jealousy and then fucking her on the desk made me starving all over again.

Oblivious to my internal machinations, she finally nodded and snagged her purse off a table by the door. "Okay, what do you want to eat?"

I slipped my hand around hers and walked beside her as she flicked the office lights off. Once we were in the hallway and she'd locked the door, she started rattling off suggestions for food. I'd never been a picky eater and truly would eat anything, so I randomly said yes to something.

When we stepped outside into a chilly rain, I hailed a cab and tugged her into it. Hours later, I lay in her bed with her silky skin warm against mine and listened to the sound of her breathing in sleep. She was usually tense, the only exceptions were when she was caught up in the madness between us or asleep, so I savored the feel of her lush body relaxed against me. I fell asleep feeling all was right with the world with the one small exception being I had no idea what do to about the fact this thing with Zoe was anything but casual.

"What?!" I blurted, promptly spewing coffee on the counter.

Ethan quickly snagged a napkin from the holder sitting against the wall and wiped up the coffee. We were sitting on the stools at my kitchen counter. He was seated to my side, angled toward me, with our knees bumping. This morning had been so good it almost hurt to think about it. Waking up beside Ethan was a little slice of heaven I'd never considered. He was always warm, as such I was warm whenever he was beside me. I'd woken to his lips and hands mapping their way down my body. He'd proceeded to leave me boneless with his fingers and mouth. I'd never thought much of oral sex. In fact, the few guys who'd bothered with it left me thinking it was a waste of time. With Ethan, I saw stars and my body scaled heights of pleasure I hadn't considered possible. Before I caught my breath, his weight was settling over me, and his cock slid into me with ease.

My body still reverberating from the echoes of my first climax, I'd rolled right into another once he set to surging into me. He'd tugged me into the shower with him and now we were having coffee before he left. It was fair to say I was completely relaxed. Up until he told me Coach Hoffman had asked him to talk with me about obtaining a new attorney to handle Ethan's charges. I spit my coffee out and now my stomach was churning.

It wasn't that I'd forgotten about this worry. I'd just shoved it out of my mind because everything happening with Ethan was too tempting and felt too good. I closed my eyes and took a breath, only to feel his hand curling into mine. The warmth and strength of it made me suddenly want to cry. I wasn't supposed to fall for him. But I had. Hard. I was in deep, and I had no idea how to get out.

I opened my eyes to find his worried gaze on me. "I told him I didn't want another attorney, so that's what we'll do," he said firmly.

I shook my head. "No, no, no. It may seem like forever ago, but this is the whole reason I tried to tell you I couldn't do this. This is my mistake, not yours. I'll call Coach Hoffman today and make some recommendations. Your case is very straightforward. We were just waiting on the court dismissal on the charges."

He shook his head firmly. "I don't want another attorney."

His haughty British accent made him sound ridiculously arrogant just now. As if he could magically wave this problem away by saying it so.

"Ethan, the mess is already made. I'm mortified that Coach Hoffman knows anything about us. I can live without being on contract for the team, but I don't want this to get out. It will look terrible for me."

"Bloody hell. Why are you worried about that? Coach won't say anything. You'll fix everything with the legal thing and then we can carry on and none of it will matter," he said, so earnestly, my heart squeezed.

I took a fortifying gulp of coffee and eyed him. "Ethan, you have to understand. If it gets out—at all—that I got involved with one of my clients, it will look bad, really bad.

Trust me, I'll get dragged through the mud. It will definitely affect my business, and I can't do that. I can make some calls and have you set up with someone I trust right away."

He muttered something else under his breath and then looked back at me, giving my hand a squeeze. "I don't like it."

"It's either that, or we stop this. Today."

I couldn't quite believe I said that, but it was the only other option.

Ethan's eyes widened and then narrowed. "No."

I couldn't help the joy that bloomed inside. I wasn't supposed to be allowing any of this to happen, but I didn't want to stop. At all.

"Okay then, you have to live with someone else being your attorney."

He glared at me before taking a gulp of coffee. "Fine. It's bloody stupid, but if it's the only way you'll keep seeing me, then that's what I'll do."

I started to free my hand from his, meaning to call Jana to ask her to make a few calls for me. I thought I might be better positioned to avoid questions about why I was handing over Ethan's case if I wasn't personally calling to ask a colleague to take over.

"You gonna let me make a phone call?" I asked, smiling slightly when he tightened his grip on my hand.

His eyes had gone dark. In a flash, the air around us was heavy. "In a sec," he said, right before he closed the distance between us and kissed me senseless.

———

The following day, I walked down the stadium hallway to meet with Coach Hoffman. He was my main point of contact for the Seattle Stars. I'd come to respect him deeply for his hands on involvement with his players and their lives. I'd seen him go to lengths to instill values in his players if he thought they were lacking. I'd been leery of accepting this retainer offer, in part because I didn't want to be anyone's lackey. There were more examples than I could count of professional sports players who were complete assholes who got off the hook legally because the wheels of justice were greased with cash and sleight of hand representation. Coach Hoffman didn't expect that of me.

As such, I wasn't feeling too great to stumble the way I had with Ethan. To be fair, Ethan could likely sweep any woman off her feet. It's just I'd thought I had more discipline, and I'd let things get away from me. I'd already handed his case over to another attorney, who was happy to take over. Jana assured me she'd spun it that I was too busy down with other matters to handle it with the white gloves it needed.

I reached Coach Hoffman's door and rapped my knuckles lightly on it. When he called for me to come in, I stepped inside, glancing to him where he sat behind his desk.

"Should I close the door?" I asked.

At his nod, I closed the door and went to sit down when he gestured to the chair across from him. He finished a phone call and spun to face me.

"Hello Zoe. It wasn't necessary for you to stop by. From what I hear, we're all set," Coach Hoffman said with a slight smile.

"Yes. I spoke with Sarah Dutton this morning. We sent the files over, and she'll finish up. Honestly, there's not much left to do," I replied. I forced myself to take a slow breath and say what I'd come here to say. "I'm aware it wasn't necessary for me to stop by, but I wanted to apologize. I shouldn't have gotten involved with Ethan while I was representing him, and for that I apologize. If you think I need to speak with team management about whether they'd like me to continue with the contract for my representation, please let me know. I..."

I started to say something else, but Coach Hoffman was shaking his head, so I stopped.

He leaned back in his chair and narrowed his eyes. He had a thoughtful, measured air about him. "Zoe, I don't really care about what happened. I only mentioned it to Ethan because I was concerned about how it might affect you if it became known you two were seeing each other. Ethan is perfectly capable of handling the blowback. But you're a very good attorney, and I know how things can be made to look bad even when they're not. As far as speaking to management, that's not necessary. I've run by them the change in his attorney, and there's nothing left to discuss. If you're worried this changes my opinion of you, it doesn't."

Relief washed through me. I'd steeled myself to deal with whatever reaction I had to face, but this was certainly the best option. "Thank you." I took a fortifying breath. "I can assure you, I don't usually let things like this happen."

Coach Hoffman's perceptive gaze held mine before he nodded slowly. "I'm aware of that." He paused and picked up a small ball off of his desk, which he proceeded to toss lightly between his hands. "You know, it's probably none of my business, but for what it's worth, it's obvious Ethan cares for you. As far as I can see, you're good for him. In fact, if I were a betting man, I'd say Ethan probably loves you. I doubt he's figured that out for himself, but there you go."

His words hit me hard—a thump to my chest with warmth blooming in my heart immediately afterwards. I couldn't quite believe what he'd just said. I had no idea what to make of it, and I wanted to jump up and down and squeal. Which, of course, I didn't do. That would've been ridiculous. I stared back at Coach Hoffman and tried to corral my wild thoughts.

"Um, I... Well, I'm not really sure what to say," I finally said.

Coach Hoffman smiled warmly and leaned his elbows on his desk, setting the ball down, only to roll it back and forth under his hand. "I probably surprised you. You know, I caught a few lucky breaks, but the best one was meeting my wife. I was a little younger than Ethan and living high on being a soccer star and traveling all over the world. That kind of life isn't very grounding. In fact, it's the opposite. Ethan has good support from his family, so he's handled it better than some. Before I heard the rumors about you two, I wondered what was up with him. I chalked it up to his brush with the law and trying to lay low. In hindsight, I think it was you. Otherwise, he'd have joked daily about the hardship of staying away from the bars. He hasn't complained once, and he's calmer and more focused than usual. Given that he's one of the best defenders I have, that's saying something. My point is a good relationship is a good thing. I still miss my wife to this day. So, in sum, I understand you feel the need to apologize for what happened, but there's an upside to everything."

I managed to nod, but the wheels in my brain were stuck on his comment that he thought Ethan loved me. I don't know what else we said over the next few minutes. My habits of polite conversation were ingrained enough that I got through it. I was saved by someone else knocking at Coach Hoffman's door. I said goodbye and walked back down the long hallway.

None of this was supposed to have happened. It terrified me to think about it, but just now I couldn't stop. I hadn't ever expected to fall in love. With anyone. Much less with a man like Ethan. He was so much more than his public image. My mind spun back to the first few times I met him. His sly, teasing manner, his cocky attitude, his insouciance so powerful it was as if he did it just to get under my skin. He was still that man, yet I now knew him to be funny and big-hearted. He spoke often of his family, not to make a point, but more in passing.

After we'd had sex without a condom for the first time—in my office!—he'd informed me later that night over takeout that his oldest sister had threatened him with bodily harm if he wasn't respectful and didn't always use a condom. He'd declared he planned to call her about it, and I begged him not to. Just thinking about it now made my cheeks hot and my heart clench as I walked to my office in the chilly drizzle.

I didn't know if what I felt for him was love, but it felt an awful lot like what I imagined it would. My own parents were still married. They'd moved to a small town in Oregon after my father retired from his prestigious law practice. He still practiced law, but on a much smaller scale. My mother had been his paralegal for as long as I could remember. They'd met in law school, and she'd finished up her paralegal coursework while she was pregnant with me. I shook my head thinking about them. For years, they'd been on me to relax and stop working so hard. Yet, they'd modeled that kind of life for me. Since they worked together, they'd never had to curtail work to spend time with each other.

I walked down the hallway to my office, wondering when I'd see Ethan again. He was a tad grumpy about me setting him up with another attorney. As often as we'd been seeing each other, we never planned ahead. I wanted to see him tonight and wondered if he had a game. Without pausing to think, I pulled out my phone and texted him.

What are you doing tonight?

Have a game. Please come.

I was smiling at the phone and then burst out laughing at his next text.

I meant that in more ways than one. ;)

The door to my office opened, and Jana poked her head around the door.

"What the hell are you laughing at?" she asked with a grin.

I flushed and quickly put my phone away. "Nothing," I replied as I walked past her into the office.

She closed the door behind us. "Okay, what's up?" she asked as she walked by me and leaned her hips on her desk.

Much as I didn't want to embarrass myself, if there was anyone who could keep me sensible, it was Jana. My lack of experience with anything resembling a serious relationship wasn't helping me. While a part of me was on cloud nine after what Coach Hoffman said about Ethan, a big part of me was worried. I hadn't meant to put my professional reputation in jeopardy, but that was the easy part. I'd already resolved it. If things continued with Ethan and it became public knowledge we were seeing each other, there might be some comments about the fact I had represented him at one point. The part that had no answer was what to do about how I felt about him and what he might want. My phone vibrated in my pocket, and I ignored it. It kept vibrating.

Jana's eyes flicked to my jacket pocket and back up. I felt my cheeks get hot again.

"Someone wants to chat. Maybe you should check on that," she said with a sly grin.

Because I knew it was Ethan, and I couldn't resist, I pulled my phone out and looked down at the screen. One look had heat rolling through me and my channel throbbing.

Did I make you blush, luv? Excellent. My next goal is to make you wet. Please come to the game tonight. I've already asked Olivia and Harper to save a seat for you. Tell me you'll be there.

I didn't even think about saying no.

I'll be there.

I couldn't bring myself to reply to his other comments. Before I managed to slide my phone back in my pocket, it buzzed in my hand.

Excellent. Wear that flippy skirt and no panties.

Butterflies rioted in my belly, and my face got so hot, I needed something to cool me down.

Since when do you tell me what to wear?

The more uptight you get, the more I like it.

Oh. My. God. He was incorrigible.

Fine. I might or might not wear that skirt. I'll definitely wear panties, so you can just forget that right now.

All I got in return was a wink emoticon. I was caught between burning desire and a goofy joy.

I'd been so absorbed in texting Ethan, I forgot I was standing beside Jana. When I looked up, she wagged her fingers at me. I blushed even harder.

"Be right back," I said before hurrying into the small restroom off the reception area.

I locked the door behind me and splashed cold water on my face and wrists. Sweet hell. Ethan was going to make me crazy. He already had. I could feel the moisture between my thighs. I was so hot and bothered, I contemplated whether I should take care of matters right now. The second that thought entered my mind, I shook my head sharply. I could not masturbate here. I had more control than that. Another splash of cold water on my face, and I held my wrists under the icy water for long enough I started to get cold. That put a damper on the need galloping through me. By the time, I returned to the reception area, Jana was behind her desk typing away.

I sat down across from her and waited until she looked my way. "Ethan's driving me crazy, and I don't know what to do," I blurted out.

One thing I loved about Jana was her focus. The second I spoke, she clicked her computer screen off and turned all of her attention to me. "Good crazy or bad crazy?" she asked.

"I don't know the difference."

She cocked her head to the side and eyed me. "Good crazy is when everything is so good it scares you. But it all feels good and nothing sneaky is going on. Bad crazy is when you're letting things keep going, but it doesn't feel good all the time, and the other person is playing games and making you want to pull your hair out. The worst kind is when you think it's good crazy, but then it turns into bad crazy. I'm very familiar with that one." She rolled her eyes and shrugged. "Anyway, which kind of crazy is it? I have a pretty good guess."

"Good crazy," I said, wishing I could will the heat away from creeping up my neck. Not for the first time, I wished my skin wasn't so fair.

Jana smiled softly. "That's what I guessed. I like Ethan. My gut tells me he's not the game playing kind of guy. He's too straightforward for that. Anyway, what do you mean you don't know what to do?"

I threw my hands up. "Just that. What do I do? I didn't... Ugh." I sighed and fiddled with the elastic cord on the corner of my hood.

Jana eyed me for a long minute, her gaze thoughtful. "I'll admit when I pushed you to dive in with him, I figured you'd finally lose your virginity—and thank fucking God you did—but I thought it would be short-lived. There's more to Ethan than meets the eye. He's coasted on his rep as a player, but he's actually a nice guy. I figured that out quick, but plenty of nice guys don't want much more than a little fun. He really likes you though."

I kept twirling the elastic cord around my finger and snapping it lightly. "So what do I do?"

Jana sighed and leaned on her elbows, resting her chin in her hand. "Seeing as it's pretty obvious you like him, why don't you relax and enjoy it?"

"Because I don't know how to do that! It all feels like more than I planned on, and I don't know what to do. I like to know what's going to happen," I said, my words trailing into a mutter.

Jana grinned. "You are definitely a planner. You can't plan love, girl."

My heart gave a swift kick, almost knocking my breath from me. Between Coach Hoffman throwing the word love out and now Jana, I didn't know what to think.

"I'm not so sure we should be talking about love just yet."

"No, you're afraid to talk about love," she countered.

When I stared back at her, wishing I could will away the churning in my stomach, she stopped grinning and took a breath.

"What I'm getting at is you can't plan emotions. If someone means a lot to you, don't run from it because you're afraid of what might go wrong. When I see the way Ethan looks at you, I'm pretty sure you're not alone."

She paused and looked over at me. "Stop it, stop being anxious over something you're making up. You like Ethan, he likes you. Enjoy it. When do you see him again?" she asked, her tone practical.

Jana knew me well, and she knew if I got stuck in a mental rut, it wouldn't be good. Focusing on something concrete nudged me out of the wheels spinning in my mind.

"I told him I'd go to his game tonight."

She grinned. "Perfect. You can be his personal cheerleader."

"I don't think they have cheerleaders," I muttered, fighting the flush creeping up my cheeks again.

"Exactly. That's why it's important for you to be there. Now go get to work. Mark Smithson called again, and I told him you'd be tied up until forever. You'd better refer him to someone else fast, or I might tell him to go to hell."

She effectively took my focus off of Ethan. "Please don't do that. I already asked Dan Connors if he'd take the case if I referred him. I ran into him at the courthouse yesterday. Dan's got more clout than me around here, so I'm sure Mark will be happy with that. I'll call his receptionist today."

Jana spun in her chair and clicked her computer screen back on. "How about you do that right away, so I don't have to listen to his smarmy voice again?"

"On it!"

I left her to whatever she was working on and made my way into my office. When I took my phone out of my jacket when I hung it up, I realized I hadn't noticed Ethan's last text.

I don't know why you insist on wearing panties when they'll get wet anyway. Save yourself the bother luv.

All it took was that little tease, and need throbbed between my thighs again. I could feel the damp silk and almost moaned.

Chapter Twenty-One

ETHAN

I walked off the field beside Alex who was in a piss poor mood because we'd lost. On one shot. It was his first missed block of the season, and I knew he was mentally attacking himself over it. I stayed quiet because I'd known Alex long enough to know he wasn't a fan of pep talks. I wasn't any happier than he was, but I could be a tad more circumspect about the whole thing. Way I saw it, we were better off losing at least once before we headed into the playoffs. I'd seen plenty of teams get cocky if they stayed undefeated during the regular season. I caught the bottle of water tossed my way as we walked by the bench and glanced up toward the team box. It was impossible for me to actually see Zoe in there, but I liked knowing she was here. Now that my focus on the pitch was turned off, all I could think about was rushing through a shower to see her.

I'd taken things a tad too far with my teasing earlier. I'd had a fucking cock stand in the locker room over it. Thank God no one happened to be around to see it.

Alex got tugged away from me for those bloody after game interviews. I might be part of our team's starting lineup, but I didn't mind at all playing a less central role than Alex or Liam. I knew Coach would chide me and remind me every player was part of a bigger puzzle. Yet, I also knew how the media saw it. Right now, they wanted to probe Alex's goalkeeper mind about the shot that slipped past his fingertips. If you asked me, they should check with the defender who was tripped by an offensive player on the other team, which kept him from blocking the shot. I knew they'd get to that, but Alex would still have to discuss how he felt. Fuck that.

With my mood not the high of winning, I was more restless than usual to see Zoe. Well, nothing was usual with her. When I wasn't at practice or playing a game, she was parked in my brain. I hurried through my shower, deflecting every naughty thought that sauntered through. I might have no shame about how much I loved women, but I'd never had to deal with worrying about getting a cock stand in the locker room. It had never even crossed my mind. My mind was on a tear though. Ever since I'd asked Zoe not to wear any panties, it was all I could think about if I had a spare moment. I hadn't had a chance to see her before the game, so I had no idea if she'd worn the skirt I'd desperately wanted her to wear. You should know, I'd never asked a woman to wear anything specific for me. In fact, I'd never thought much about what a woman wore. With Zoe, I noticed everything.

I threw on my clothes snagged my phone to check it on my way to find Zoe. Only to discover a text from her first.

I saved myself the bother.

For a beat, I was confused. Saved herself the bother? Of what? Then, I recalled my last text telling her to save herself the bother of wearing panties. Fuck me. That's all it took, and blood shot straight to my groin. Zoe had me wrapped around her finger, and she had no idea how much power she had over me.

I was almost running down the hall when I heard my

name. I spun back to see Tristan behind me. He caught up to me in seconds.

"What's the rush, mate?" he asked.

I had too much pride to admit I'd been running to find Zoe as fast as I could, so I shrugged.

"Liam's rounding us up for dinner. He thinks Alex needs a few beers," Tristan continued.

Bloody hell. I couldn't bow out of that. We often got together after games. Usually, I was an easy yes. But I wanted to see Zoe. Now. And I didn't want company. I was formulating some kind of excuse when I heard my name and glanced to where I'd been running to see Zoe walking between Olivia and Harper.

She was wearing that black skirt that swung around her knees with tall black boots. Fuck me. Now I knew she had nothing on underneath that skirt, and all I wanted was to find a place where I could bend her over and sink inside of her. Instead, I was in the stadium hallway and voices were coming our way from the other side as well. I did some fast talk in my mind to get my cock back to half-mast. That was as good as I could get for now.

Next thing I knew, we were moving as a group toward a diner nearby. Harper had announced Alex liked the place, so that's where we were going. Zoe walked beside me, and it took every ounce of restraint I had not to slide my hand down over her bottom. If I did that, I didn't think I could control myself. I made do with holding onto her hand as if my life depended on it.

She seemed unaffected and chatted graciously with Harper and Olivia about something they must've started talking about before. I had no idea what it was because I was busy trying not to have a cock stand. I was usually the master of fun and games and never one to lose control, but I could barely keep my shit together around Zoe.

I breathed a sigh of relief once we were seated in the diner in a giant booth in the corner with Zoe pushed up

beside me. Perfect. Tristan was across from me, his perceptive gaze flicking from me to Zoe, but he didn't tease. In
fact, he ended up being distracted by Daisy who was mashed
between him and Olivia. I distantly wondered what was up
with them, but didn't think much of it. Daisy was plenty
beautiful with her blonde hair, wide brown eyes and curves
that went of forever. At one time, I'd had it in my head I
should go after her. But there was no spark there. In fact,
Daisy had announced I felt like the brother she never had.
Seeing as she felt like a fifth sister to me, we'd laughed about
it and stayed friends ever since.

Once drinks were served and conversation was meandering, I couldn't resist sliding my hand between Zoe's thighs. I
bit back a grin when I heard her breath hitch. Good. She
could suffer as much as me. It's not that I doubted her when
she implied she hadn't worn her panties, but I was still jolted
when I pushed the soft fabric of her skirt out of the way and
discovered she definitely was *not* wearing any. The inside of
her thighs were damp.

Nudging her knees apart just barely, I stroked a finger
through her folds. I expected her to resist, but she didn't.
The feel of her got me so hard, I almost stopped. Almost.
With us tucked in the corner and the table completely
hiding anything my hands were doing, I set out to tease her.
It was additionally convenient to have her skirt shielding my
hand from anyone who happened to look down at her lap.

"Eh, well, Ethan's the one who got that speeding ticket,"
Liam said, his eyes catching mine with a wink.

I knew I'd better manage to converse or the fact I was
trying to drive Zoe wild might become obvious.

"I wasn't going that fast," I countered with a grin. I
honestly had no fucking clue what Liam was talking about.
But I had gotten a few speeding tickets in my lifetime, so I
could play along.

Olivia pursed her lips and nudged Liam with her elbow.
"Stop deflecting. I bet you got more speeding tickets than

Ethan. My point was our car insurance went up again because you got another ticket. That's all," she said with a low laugh and a roll of her eyes.

"Right luv. I was just trying to say I'm not the only bloke who speeds," Liam said with another grin thrown my way.

I shrugged just as I sank a finger knuckle deep into Zoe. Liam said something else, and I managed an answer. I was relieved when he turned his attention to Tristan and chided him for spending too much time studying. I glanced to Zoe and saw her cheeks were flushed a pretty pink. I loved when she flushed because her freckles stood out then. Her channel throbbed around my finger, and I beat back the urge to make her come right there. I wanted to, bloody hell did I want to, but more than that I wanted to tease her to madness.

Dinner carried on. I occasionally toyed with Zoe—stretching her and savoring her slick heat on my fingers. I teased light circles around her clit with my thumb and loved how flushed she was. Every so often, her breath would catch. At some point, she reached down and tried to nudge my hand away. This was in the midst of a light-hearted argument between Daisy and Tristan.

When I felt her hand against mine, I grabbed it and held it still. I knew she wouldn't want it to be obvious and start wrestling me right here at the table. I leaned over, just close enough so only she could hear me.

"I want you to touch yourself."

Her eyes whipped to me and away. "We're in public. No," she whispered fiercely.

I scanned the table. No one was paying a bit of attention to us. The waiter had arrived and was stacking empty plates. Liam was jabbering on about something, Alex looked plain tired, and Tristan was caught up in whatever he was talking about with Daisy. In short, we might as well have been alone.

Zoe's pulse fluttered in her neck, and her breath came in

short little pants. Even though she'd just tried to dissuade me, she didn't move her hand away.

"You are so fucking wet. I bet you played with yourself earlier," I murmured.

I was out of my fucking mind, and I didn't even care. I wanted to know she was as lost and adrift in this madness as I was.

I forced myself to drag my fingers out of her. It was almost painful, but I managed. I glanced to her. The sight of her flushed cheeks and the knowledge of how wet she was had me hard as a rock. What she did next nearly made me lose it. I felt her hand shift and her finger slide through her folds. She bit her lip and a little sigh escaped. She quickly moved her hand away and glanced to me.

"I can't. I'm too close," she murmured.

"Too close to what?"

She glared at me. I looked away to scan the table again. Alex was getting up and saying something to Liam.

"To what?" I repeated.

"Oh my God. You know exactly what I'm talking about," she said with a huff.

Then, she pushed my hand away and snapped her knees together.

Oh yes. Game on.

Chapter Twenty-Two

ZOE

The door to my apartment slammed shut behind us. I was in a fog of need. My entire body was thrumming with it and had been for hours. It's a miracle I didn't have an orgasm right there at the diner. I managed to walk halfway normally across the room and flick on a lamp. I felt Ethan come up behind me. His hands slid down my hips. A prickle of heat raced down my spine. His lips landed on my neck with hot, wet kisses while he dragged my skirt up.

I could feel his cock—hot and hard through the denim of his jeans pressing against my bare bottom. The friction of the rough fabric against my skin was unbearably arousing. My pulse was racing wildly, and I could hardly catch my breath.

"I meant to drag this out, but I don't think I can."

His lips moved against my ear, his breath gusting across the sensitive skin there. The gruff whisper was enough to nearly send me over the edge. We were standing on the far side of the living room where I'd gone to flick on the light. Thank God there was a wall beside us because I nearly collapsed when he spread my cheeks and dragged a finger down to dip into my folds.

I moaned, and my knees buckled, my palm slapping against the wall to catch my balance. Everything blurred. I dimly heard the sound of a zipper and then felt the hot velvety skin of his cock against me. He teased me, dragging the head of his cock back and forth through my slippery folds. I'd been wet for hours now, on edge with my control shredded.

"Ethan, please..." I murmured, my voice pleading.

I couldn't even recognize who I was. Out of control with need pounding through me so hard, everything narrowed to the intensity of this moment. I cried out when he sank inside me. He surged in hard and fast, filling me completely in one stroke. I leaned both hands to the wall and arched back as he began to rock into me. One of his hands gripped my hip, his fingers digging in. The other slid up my back in a heated pass. He wound my hair around his hand and tugged lightly on it, pulling me into each stroke. I was so close, it was mere seconds before pleasure lashed me like a whip, hitting me so hard I'd have collapsed if he weren't there to hold me up.

I heard his rough cry mingling amidst my own and the heat of his release fill me. Our breath heaved together. My pulse gradually slowed, and he eased his grip on my hair. He drew out and spun me around, pressing me against the wall and kissing me. This kiss wasn't like most of our kisses. Oh, it was wet, and it was deep, yet it felt as if he was sinking into me. He kissed me with slow strokes, gentle nips and dusted kisses along my jawline before coming back to my lips. Soft shudders wracked me, echoes of my orgasm. When he drew away, his eyes met mine. What I saw in his gaze took my breath away and set my heart to pounding again. He brushed a loose lock of hair off of my forehead.

Without a word, he lifted me into his arms and carted me into the bathroom. I wasn't accustomed to being carried.

Being as tall as most of them, that wasn't a surprise. I'd never have guessed I'd enjoy it, but because it was Ethan I did. He did it so easily and held me close against him. I'd have happily stayed there, but I didn't mind him peeling my clothes off and dropping his to the floor before tugging me into the shower with him.

Drifting into sleep later, I should've been wondering all kinds of things, but I wasn't. It felt too good to be curled up against his heat and strength and feel his fingers sliding through my hair.

Chapter Twenty-Three

ETHAN

"Excuse me?" I asked Sarah Dutton.

Sarah glanced up from a document she'd been reading on her desk. "I'm not sure why, but Ted Duncan's saying now he'd like to meet again. He'll be here in a minute."

"Didn't you just tell me the charges were formally dropped yesterday?" I countered, instantly annoyed she saw fit to think I needed to sit through another meeting.

She nodded and adjusted her glasses. "I did, but it's good form to follow up with a meeting request, so we will."

Sarah was my new attorney, the one Zoe *made* me accept. I still wasn't happy about that. Sarah was nice enough and was even pretty with her shiny blonde hair. I objectively considered I might've been interested in her once upon a time. She was on the flashy side for an attorney. As the case had been ever since I'd first kissed Zoe, no other woman had any attraction for me. All I could do was dispassionately notice them. I was fairly certain a woman could walk around bare ass naked in front of me, and I wouldn't be tempted. Unless the woman in question was Zoe. With her, she could wear a shapeless sack, and I'd want her.

I'd had it in mind I'd show up this morning and walk out
of here with this finally behind me. Now, Sarah was telling
me I had to meet with the other guy's attorney. I couldn't
wait for it to be over.

Within minutes, Ted Duncan was lumbering his way into
Sarah's office. I'd had the displeasure of meeting him once
before. He was a blowhard if I ever met one, all bluff and
gruff and loud. We were seated at a small circular table in a
conference room at Sarah's office. Ted sat down across from
me, making an ungodly amount of noise for a man taking a
seat. He thunked a briefcase on the table, adjusted and read-
justed the height of his chair and somehow managed to
catch his sleeve on the arm. Sarah quietly kept her eyes
trained on some papers in front of her. Far as I could tell,
she wasn't reading a damn thing. My guess was she knew
Ted's routine and was waiting for him to be done making a
mini-ruckus.

Blessedly, Ted finally leaned back in his chair and glanced
from me to Sarah. "Well, thank you for taking time to meet
with me."

Sarah only now looked up and adjusted her glasses on her
nose. "Of course, Ted. The court formally dismissed the
charges yesterday. I'm not sure what you were hoping to
discuss today."

Ted cleared his throat and looked over at me. "Perhaps
Mr. Walsh could fill you in."

My gut tightened. I had a clue where he might be going
with this, and I didn't like it. Not one bit. "Pardon?" I asked.

"I don't suppose you consider it a problem you were
involved with Ms. Lawson the entire time she was representing you," Ted said, barely concealing the smarmy gleam
in his eyes.

I'd done a bit of my homework here and knew the one
tiny detail that kept Zoe on the right side of the ethics was
the fact I'd kissed her before she became my attorney. Now,
I knew we hadn't been 'involved,' but as far as I was

concerned, that kiss met the standard of commencing our sexual relationship before her representation of me. In any other setting, I'd likely laugh about it. But right now. I was red hot furious. I opened my mouth to say something, only to pause when Sarah cut right in.

"Ted, that is completely irrelevant," she said, her voice crisp and clear. "These charges were dismissed due to the fact *your* client punched my client first. The police made it clear that after they reviewed the security video they had no grounds to charge Mr. Walsh when your client initiated the interaction. As to your implied threat, I know Ms. Lawson very well. She and Mr. Walsh were..."

The slightest hesitation occurred, and I jumped in. "We were involved before she took my case," I said firmly, leaning heavy on the haughty. I was so bloody mad, I wanted to lean across the table and shake Ted Duncan with his rumpled hair and smarmy presence.

Sarah seemed to sense I was about agitated and placed her hand on my arm. "Thank you, Ethan. I was about to say the same thing." She squeezed my forearm slightly. I supposed it was her polite way of telling me to shut the hell up. So I did.

She looked straight across the table at Ted. "Nothing improper there. As you know, attorneys can and do represent those with whom they're involved as long as it began before the course of the case. What is your point in bringing this up, Ted?"

He adjusted the lapels of his jacket and huffed. "Whether or not it meets some silly standard doesn't change the fact it looks improper. My point in bringing it up is simply that. If you'd prefer I keep this quiet, then you might want to consider agreeing to a settlement with my client."

Bloody fucking hell. I saw red. I was about to stand and reach across the table to yank Ted-fucking-Duncan out of his chair. Sarah put her hand on my arm again, and damn did she have an iron grip.

"Ted, that sounds an awful lot like extortion to me," she said, her voice clear and commanding.

Ted's face reddened. "Now Sarah, that's not what I meant. I'm just saying that it won't look good for anyone to misunderstand Zoe's relationship with Mr. Walsh here."

"There is nothing to misunderstand, you fucking asshole," I said, cutting in even though I knew Sarah preferred me to keep my mouth shut. "You can pretend like that wasn't blackmail, but it bloody was and you know it. If you dare to start throwing dirt around about Zoe, I'll make your life hell."

I didn't wait to hear what he said and shook Sarah's hand off my arm before storming out of the conference room. It was either that, or I'd pummel Ted's face.

I fumed as I stalked out of the building and nearly sprinted down the street to Zoe's office. I didn't know what the hell she'd want to do about what the bloody jerk had just implied, but I figured she'd want to know.

I slowed to a walk when I entered the reception area of her office. Odd, but I relaxed the second I walked in there. Solely because I knew I was about to see Zoe. Jana glanced up from her desk and held a finger up.

Jana nodded along with whomever she was speaking to and said, "Ms. Lawson is tied up in meetings for the rest of the day. She's already clarified her decision about your case, but I'll pass on your message." She tapped a button and ended the call before looking over at me and rolling her eyes. "That was the asshole Mark. He's not happy Zoe isn't taking his case. He'll get over it," she said with a shrug.

I stepped to her desk. "Tell me something, what do you think Zoe would do if she knows it's out that we've been seeing each other?"

"I didn't know it was a secret," Jana said with a puzzled glance at me.

I quickly summarized the meeting with Sarah and Ted. It took no more than a minute, and Jana looked furious.

"Fucking Ted Duncan. He's such a sleaze bag. Of course that was extortion. Ted's such a shithead, he'll find a way to spread rumors anyway."

She stared at me for a few beats. "You think you have to tell Zoe about this, don't you?"

"Of course." I paused and bit back a groan. This was exactly what Zoe had been worried about, and I'd dismissed it. Truth was, I could get away with all kinds of things, so I tended not to care. I couldn't have known that pursuing her wouldn't be just a brief thing. I couldn't have known I'd feel the way I did now—worried and concerned for her and ready to kick some guy's ass. My chest felt tight, and my head hurt.

Jana sighed and ran a hand through her wild hair. I never knew what to expect with her, and today she had blue streaks in it, layered atop the purple already there. "Zoe's going to completely freak out, but you'd better tell her. If you don't, she'll freak out worse."

"I know, I know. Fuck." I tapped the toe of my shoe against the edge of her desk and eyed her. "You just said she was tied up all day. When...?"

Jana flashed a grin. "Oh, I was screening. He's an asshole, so she's always busy when he calls. Don't go thinking she asked me to do that. I choose to take the initiative for pricks like him. Anyway, go on back."

I stepped into Zoe's office, pausing once I closed the door behind me. Her back was to the door as she looked at something on her computer screen. Her rich auburn hair was swirled into a tidy knot. All she had to do was hide her hair like that, and it made me want to undo it and untidy her in every way possible.

"Did you hear back from...?"

Her question trailed off as she spun in her chair and saw me. I presumed she'd figured I was Jana. Her surprise morphed into a slow smile. Bloody hell. This woman was going to kill me. A smile. Nothing but a smile, and I got hard. Much as I wanted to lock the door behind me and have another naughty interlude in her office, I had to deliver the bad news and hopefully get her not to freak out.

"Hey, I didn't know you were stopping by," she said.

I walked quickly and sat down in the chair across from her. Never one to wait, I blurted out, "Ted Duncan knows we were seeing each other when you were representing me." I elected not to elaborate further about his implied threat about a settlement. I figured I could talk with Sarah first before we worried more about that.

Zoe's eyes widened and her face blanched. She sat completely still for a moment and then shook her head sharply. "Oh my God. This is what I was afraid of."

She picked up a pen and started flipping it rapidly back and forth.

"Don't let him bully you, Zoe. Let me deal with him," I said.

I had no idea what I meant to do, but I'd stand in front of a moving train to keep her from being harmed. I also fucking hated Ted Duncan.

Zoe was quiet. Too quiet. Her cheeks were splotchy red. All those times I loved watching her flush were nothing like this moment. She was clearly distressed, and I wanted to make it go away. Now.

I stood and started to round the desk. She waved me away.

"No, no. Just... Let me think." She put her face in her hands and took a shaky breath.

I couldn't help myself and took a step toward her again. She dropped her hands and lasered me with a glare. "Stop it. This is how this all started. I told you I couldn't do this and you kept coming at me."

Her words hit me in the gut. They fucking hurt. Oh, they were true all right, but the way she made it sound sullied it. I stared back at her. I admit, I wasn't in the calmest state of mind. Hell, I was idling on the edge of the anger fucking Ted Duncan had set off, and it pissed me off to have her upset like this. Intellectually, I knew she had a point. I'd pushed. Because I wanted her that fucking bad. But it was more than that. I knew it, and I hoped she knew it too.

"Zoe, it wasn't like that. You know..."

"Yes it was! I told you precisely why I shouldn't let it happen. I'm not mad at you. I'm mad at myself. I knew better, and I fell right into it anyway."

She stood abruptly. "You have to go."

"Why do I have to go?"

My head felt like it was going to explode. I couldn't take the look on Zoe's face. Her eyes were shuttered, and she looked angry and frightened at once. I tried to reach for her as she stepped past me.

"Zoe, luv. Let me help with this. You don't have to..."

She spun back, her eyes snapping. "You can't help. You'll be fine no matter what. I can't have rumors circulating that I fuck my clients. When it comes to stuff like that, it's a one-way street. What men can get away with ruins women's careers. I should've stopped this, hell I never should've let it start. For now, I can't see you. You have to go and let me figure this out on my own. If I have any chance to shut this off, it won't happen if I'm still seeing you."

It was like static in my brain. I couldn't think over the buzzing. Meanwhile, my heart was pounding so hard, it physically hurt. She didn't wait and spun around, walking briskly through her door. I meant to follow her and tell her she couldn't do this. I didn't care what Jana saw or heard. But when I got out to the waiting area, fucking Ted Duncan was standing there with a pasted on smarmy smile. I didn't even think and walked straight up to him and punched him. I have no fucking idea when Tristan had showed up or how he even knew where I was, but he came walking in right after I clocked Ted in the face.

Zoe's face was sheet white.

Tristan bodily shoved me out of the way. "Back the fuck off, mate. What are you thinking?"

Ted was swearing and muttering something about calling the police. Jana stood up and got in his face. "What the fuck do you think you're pulling, Ted? You think you can blackmail Zoe and Ethan? Go right ahead and try."

Zoe, Tristan, and I swung to stare at Jana. Jana didn't break free from her stare down with Ted. Let me tell you, it was quite the sight to see her with her wild hair and her usually friendly demeanor pissed off.

Jana waited a few beats and then glanced from him to me. "Let me guess, you'd like to make a little more trouble in case you can sleaze someone into paying you off to shut up? You're the last fucking attorney who should be spouting off about ethics. You forget how much I know about you from where I used to work. I might've left under less than ideal circumstances, but I know exactly who to call if I want to stir shit up. Here's the deal: you shut up and leave, or I'll make a few calls. Right here. Right now."

The quiet in the office was heavy. After a tense moment, Ted nodded. He didn't say a word and turned and left.

Zoe looked at Jana. "What the hell was that about?"

"Before he went out on his own, Ted worked at the same firm I did. He left after he got caught screwing one of the interns. She was legal, but just barely. Might not seem like much to hold over him, but his ex got a shitty deal in their divorce because he managed to keep this and a bunch of other shit about his hidden accounts out of court. He won't want any of that to become public."

Jana flounced back to her desk and sat down, her eyes flicking from me to Zoe before she looked to Tristan. "Hi Tristan, thanks for stopping by," she said brightly.

"Why the hell *are* you here?" I asked him.

"Your sister showed up, and I told her I'd track you down," he said with a shrug.

"What? Which one?"

"Belle," he said simply.

I had no idea why Belle was here. She was my youngest

sister and tended toward carefree and bubbly. It wasn't a shock for her to show up unannounced, but it wasn't common either.

"Okay," I said slowly. "Mind telling her I'll be there shortly?"

I didn't want to walk out of here without talking to Zoe. I glanced over to her, not even bothering to wait for Tristan's reply.

She was already turning away. "I have to go," she said, striding quickly back into her office.

I was hot on her heels. "Zoe, can we talk?"

I reached for her hand, and she shook me off. "Not now. I can't talk now, Ethan. You just punched a colleague of mine. Maybe Jana's right, and she can get him to keep his mouth shut, but it's not just him I have to worry about. I can't keep doing this."

Her words tumbled out staccato and sharp. She didn't even look at me as she grabbed her purse and jacket. I could barely think over the static in my brain and the pounding of my heart.

Before I had a chance to form a sentence, she was dashing out of the office. I started to race after her when Jana's voice brought me up short.

"Let her go for now, Ethan."

I spun back in the open doorway. "But I..."

She cut me off. "It's obvious you want to talk to her. Hell, it's obvious you love her. Trust me on this. Zoe's stubborn. She doesn't take well to being pressured. Let her cool off first. I'll talk to her. Maybe you don't see it, but she's right about worrying about this thing with you two getting out the wrong way. I'll admit I told her to go for it, but then I'm the same woman who blew my career up over getting involved with the wrong guy. I don't think you're the wrong guy, but I'm a romantic at heart. Go see your sister, and try again tomorrow with Zoe."

I stared at Jana. I felt like my head was going to explode

and my heart was going to pound its way out of my chest. Tristan's voice punctured the turmoil in my mind.

"She's right, mate. Let it rest. You can tell Belle all about it, and she'll tell you what to do," he said with a wry grin.

Because I didn't know what else to do, I followed Tristan home, barely recalling I'd just punched a man over Zoe. I didn't even penetrate my brain that I was that lost and out of control. Over a woman. Instead of worrying over that, all I could think about was the shuttered expression on Zoe's face.

Chapter Twenty-Four

ZOE

The rain fell heavily as I walked briskly down the street, huddled in my raincoat and wishing I could will away everything that had happened this afternoon. A horn blared in the street, and I glanced up, realizing I was about to walk by the entrance to Sarah's office building. Ever since Ethan had dropped the little bomb that Ted knew about us, my thoughts had been spinning. I was so angry with myself for letting anything happen with him. I'd known better. Back when I had a little will to resist, I should've hung on. Instead, I'd let myself get swept into the vortex of him. Once the boundaries had been crossed, I hadn't even tried to keep it from unfolding. As a result, I was mortified. Ethan's quick assurances that he could somehow make it better only served to annoy me. He had no idea. I'd worked so hard to get where I was professionally and now it was all at risk. All over sex. That's it. Sex and nothing more. I had no idea what I'd been thinking, but I was flat out crazy to think there was more to Ethan and me.

Don't beat yourself and him up over this. For God's sake, don't go and make it worse by telling everyone. You love Ethan, and there's a really good chance he loves you too.

Right. Don't be stupid.

Variations of this little debate had been circling in my brain ever since I'd dashed out of the office. There was my stupid heart. My incredibly stupid heart that dove right into this mess with Ethan on the coattails of the wild, thrumming desire that drew me to him in the first place. Then, there was my mind. My mind that had gotten me pretty far in life with careful planning and keeping me sheltered from the messiness of relationships. My mind had turned out to be a weak foe against overwhelming desire and my fanciful heart falling for Ethan. It all would have been so much simpler if he were the man he appeared to be on the surface—a shallow, insouciant player who was out for nothing more than a little fun.

Instead, he was so much more. My heart ached, and I didn't know what to do. So I did what made the most sense. I'd come clean with a few trusted colleagues and figure out what to do. Maybe what happened with Ethan and I wasn't ethical, but I'd transferred his case as I should've, and I was ending things now.

I flipped my hood back once I stepped through the doors into the office building and gave my jacket a shake. Within moments, I exited the elevator and entered Sarah's office. Sarah and I had gone to law school together, along with Jana before she took time out from school to help take care of her sister. Sarah was an excellent attorney, and I trusted her. I knew she'd be honest with me about what she thought, but she wouldn't gab about it.

Her receptionist took my name, and I sat down to wait. Fishing my phone out of my pocket, I glanced at the screen to see a wall of texts from Ethan. My heart clenched. I didn't want to read them, but I couldn't help myself.

Jana told me to leave you alone for now. If you're wondering, I don't fucking want to. When can I see you? We need to talk.

Ten minutes later.

My sister Belle wants to meet you. Where are you?

Ten minutes later.

I'm sure you're freaking out, but it will be fine. Jana says she can handle Ted, and I'll kick his ass if I have to. Again.

I couldn't help but laugh a little, a bitter, sad laugh. I knew Jana would do battle for me. I wasn't quite so sure how to feel about the curl of warmth that filtered around my heart knowing Ethan wanted to protect me too. I was used to standing on my own. By myself. I'd never thought of that as lonely, but right now it felt like it.

Another ten minutes between texts.

Luv, you're killing me here. Please tell me where you are, so I don't have to come find you. Belle and Tristan are worried now too.

Another ten minutes.

I know you're in a different spot than me, so it looks different, but it'll be fine.

Another few minutes.

Bloody hell. Where are you?

That was the last text from him, sent just a few minutes ago. I'd completely forgotten the unexpected arrival of his sister and wondered what that was about. I wanted to meet her. For all the wrong reasons. I wanted to know that part of his life because it was so obvious his family meant a lot to him. But that wasn't who he was to me. I couldn't keep letting my silly heart and body lead me down this path of insanity. As it was, I was facing professional mortification over getting involved with him. I'd already been stupid enough.

"Zoe, come on back."

I glanced up to see Sarah standing in the doorway to her office, gesturing for me to come in. Once I was there, I plunked down in the chair across from her, feeling a bit like a weary, drowned rat. My skirt was damp and water dripped off my raincoat to the floor.

"I meant to call you," Sarah said, her concerned gaze scanning my face.

For a minute, I was puzzled and then I put the pieces together. Ethan had been here at her office when Ted dropped his little bit of news.

"I'm guessing you think I'm an idiot," I finally said.

Sarah shook her head quickly. "Not at all. Ted Duncan's an asshole. Ethan took off, so I didn't get a chance to fill him in, but I made it clear to Ted if he tried to spread any rumors, I'd report him to the licensing board. Don't even start worrying about this, okay?"

I forced myself to take a breath. My chest felt tight and my head was pounding. I didn't like how this entire situation had spiraled out of my control. None of this would've happened if I hadn't gotten involved with Ethan. I looked over at Sarah whose expression was nothing but kind.

"It's easy for you to say. I made a mess of this. I know I shouldn't have let anything happen. It just doesn't feel good to have Ted knowing this. He's such a..."

"Zoe, stop beating yourself. Ethan said you two were involved before you took his case. I thought he was going to climb across the table and kick Ted's ass."

I rolled my eyes. "Well, when Ted showed up at my office, Ethan hauled off an hit him."

Sarah's eyes widened. "Oh God. Did Ted call the police?"

I shook my head and quickly summarized what Jana said to him. "You know Jana, she'll think she has it all handled. No matter what, Ted can make things uncomfortable for me."

Sarah shook her head slowly. "Stop it. Ted has a crappy reputation because he's a living, breathing example of an ambulance chaser. So what if people find out you and Ethan are involved? You did actually transfer his case. Technically, I think you didn't have to, but you did anyway. This line of thinking is going to make you crazy."

"Trust me, I *know* I should've known better, but it

happened and now I'm trying to clean up the mess. You know how it is. If people hear I got involved with a client, it won't look good," I muttered, my cheeks flaming.

Sarah leaned back in her chair and brushed her hair off her shoulders. Like me, Sarah had put a lot of work into building her career. She was bright and sharp. A big difference between us was she married her college sweetheart and already had two kids. She drummed her fingers on the table.

I took a breath and let it out, anxious because she didn't say anything more. "I should've transferred the case sooner, but nothing much was happening for a bit on it. I, well, I wasn't thinking too clearly."

Sarah grinned. "Kinda hard to do with a man like Ethan Walsh. He's dreamy and has that sexy British accent. It's obvious he adores you." When I didn't return her grin, she cocked her head to the side, her gaze sobering.

"Please tell me he didn't talk about us."

"Oh no, it wasn't like that. Before that thing with Ted, he kept saying what a great attorney you were, and he hoped I would do just as good of a job. I didn't have much to do, so I assured him it would be fine. It's not like he said much, more that the way he talked about you, it was obvious he thinks you're amazing. Because it was you and I had no idea, I figured he had the hots for you and nothing more, so..." Her words trailed off with a shrug.

I was so bad off about Ethan, this tiny sliver offered me a ticket to wishful thinking and fantasyland. I gave myself a shake and looked over at Sarah. I could not go there. "That's nice and all, but what the hell should I do about Ted?"

"Nothing. Don't take his bait. Whether Jana can keep him shut up or not, I don't think you need to worry as much as you are. If I hear anything, I'll report him to the board for threatening you like that. I know you're worried about your end of things, but Ted was trying to extort a settlement from Ethan over this. That's an actual legal problem. Maybe you got involved with a client, but you did the right thing and handed his case over. Plus, Ethan's the only one who could really cause trouble for you, and he claims it started before you took his case. I think you should stop worrying and let it go. I've got your back and so do plenty of people."

I didn't like her answer, mostly because I hated how I felt. I was mortified at ending up in this situation because it just wasn't the kind of thing I did. Hell, before I met Ethan, I was a virgin. That's how far away from this kind of thing I'd been. I looked over at Sarah with a sigh. "I was hoping you'd have a better suggestion."

Sarah smiled ruefully. "I think you're making it out as more than it needs to be."

"Fine." I stood and adjusted my raincoat. I started to turn away when Sarah said my name again.

"What?"

"Is it serious with Ethan?" she asked.

My heart clenched and my mind spun back to the other night when he'd kissed me against the wall. I'd felt like we were alone in the universe, caught in a shimmering web of intimacy with every fiber of me stitching tighter and tighter to him.

I don't know what she saw in my expression, but her eyes softened and she stood, rounding her desk quickly and pulling me into a hug. She stepped back, cupping her hands on my arms and squeezing.

"No matter what, you'll be fine. If he means that much, don't let this chance slip away."

My mouth fell open before I snapped it shut. "I didn't say that," I blurted out.

Sarah smiled softly and stepped back. "The look on your face said it all." She paused, her gaze considering. "You told me way back when I married Jack that I was a romantic. Maybe I am, but the thing is, we don't always get to be with someone we love. I know you're all about being practical, and I respect the hell out of you. But if you love this guy—

and my gut tells me you do—don't let this stupid thing get in the way."

Blessedly, her receptionist rapped on the door and poked her head around it. "Your five o'clock is here," she said.

Sarah nodded, and I made my escape. There were all kinds of things I didn't want to think about right now. Contemplating how much Ethan had come to mean to me the same day I was facing the magnitude of my poor judgment was simply too much. I gave a wave and headed back out into the rainy evening.

A bit later, I reached the entrance to my apartment building and hesitated. Ethan had texted a few more times, his last one indicating he planned to come look for me. I didn't know what to do about any of it, but I knew if I saw him it would only muddy the waters. He was too powerful of a draw for me, and I needed to think clearly. Instead of going inside, I headed around the corner to the parking garage and hopped in my rarely used car.

Chapter Twenty-Five

ETHAN

"Oh my God! You're in love!" Belle squealed. She looked from me to Tristan, her brown eyes wide with glee. "Isn't it great?"

Tristan, good mate that he was, barely nodded and appeared thoroughly absorbed in a sci-fi movie on the telly. Belle was seated between us on the sectional couch and swung to look back at me.

"It's about time. I'm so happy. You need to do something big now," she declared, her honey-blonde ponytail bouncing up and down.

I wasn't quite sure how my little sister had come to this conclusion, but she had. Thing was, I was in a pissy mood and had been since yesterday when Zoe took off from her office. I still didn't really know why Belle had shown up unannounced. She'd given me some breezy explanation about missing me, her only brother, and needing a change of pace. Under normal circumstances, I'd want to know more, but I was fit to be tied because I couldn't reach Zoe. She'd ignored all of my texts and wasn't home. Last night, I'd barely slept. This morning Belle kept asking how come I kept checking my phone, so I finally mentioned Zoe. Belle was like a dog with a bone, so she'd kept at it until I explained the mini-fiasco of yesterday.

Apparently, the whole story led her to conclude I was in love. Merely thinking the word made my heart give a hard thump. I swallowed against the tightness in my chest and wondered where the hell Zoe was. I couldn't think about my feelings when the more pressing matter was Zoe's whereabouts and making sure she saw reason and didn't try to shut me out. Once I solved that, I could ponder this whole love thing.

"Belle, what the bloody hell do you mean?" I asked.

She hooked a foot under her knee and sighed. "It sounds like she's stressing out and doesn't know if it's worth everything to be with you. So you must show her."

Tristan flicked a glance to Belle. "Everything?" he asked, his tone droll.

Belle blew her breath out, effectively blowing a lock of hair out of her eyes. "Yes, everything. I mean, her career is on the line."

"Her career is not on the fucking line," I muttered.

Belle had a tendency toward drama. She was overly romantic. Most of the time, it was amusing. Right now, I wasn't finding it so.

She must've sensed my low threshold for annoyance because her gaze softened. Twirling the end of her ponytail around her index finger, she eyed me. "Well, maybe it's not, but it sounds like she's worried. I think you should call Jana and make sure that Ted jerk is taken care of. Then, we can find Zoe."

"Not a bad plan," Tristan said with a sage nod.

I stared at him and then looked to Belle.

"We?"

She nodded, a tad too enthusiastically. "Yes, I'm here to help."

"Oh, so that's why you're here?" I countered with a roll of my eyes. "I'll go with the first part of your plan though."

I slipped my phone out and called Zoe's office. I couldn't help but hope Jana would tell me Zoe was there today. Once she answered, I jumped in.

"You wouldn't happen to know where Zoe is?" I asked.

"Ethan, oh my God. I'm so glad you called. She asked me to give you a message, but she forgot to get me your number. If you were worried about the team staff giving out your contact info, you can rest easy knowing they absolutely will not. I called over there, and they got all uptight on me," Jana said with a little huff.

"Is Zoe there?"

My heart set to thudding against my ribs and that knot of tension in my gut started to ease. Until Jana spoke.

"No, hon. She's not. She told me to tell you not to worry, and she's at her parents' for a day or two."

I sat in silence, wrestling with a mix of disappointment, anger and frustration. I needed to see Zoe, and she was making it really difficult for that to happen.

"Don't suppose you'd tell me where her parents are?"

Jana's sigh came through the line. "I can't. I want to, but I promised Zoe I wouldn't, and she's my best friend."

"Fuck."

"Oh Ethan. She'll be back soon, and you can straighten everything out."

Much as I wanted to badger Jana into telling me how to find Zoe, I sensed it would be futile. I turned my attention to the one thing I could try to resolve.

"Since I can't do a bloody thing about that, let's you and I sort this mess she's worried about. Does she need to be as worried as she is?"

"No and yes. No, because she technically didn't do anything wrong. Attorney's getting involved with their clients isn't a legal problem. If the relationship started before she took your case, there's not even an issue."

I couldn't resist cutting in. "It did."

Jana laughed softly. "I suppose it did if you're counting that time you kissed her."

"I am," I said firmly. Because I'd been obsessed with Zoe straight through ever since, so as far as I was concerned that was the truth.

Jana continued, "That doesn't mean people don't gossip about stuff like that. She's worried because she has a really good professional reputation, and she feels like she messed up. The thing is, that's why she transferred your case. The reason she might need to worry is how things get twisted. Ted Duncan is a class-A jerk. I talked to Sarah today. Between the dirt I have on him and Sarah being present for his little blackmail threat, I don't think you need to worry."

I had all kinds of things to say, but most of them were pointless at the moment. I asked the main question, "Are you sure he won't hang this over Zoe's head?"

"No. My guess is she'll probably come clean with whoever she's made up in her head she needs to."

Precisely what I was worried about.

"If you talk to her, tell her not to do that."

Jana laughed softly. "Boy, you've got it bad. I've already told her that, but I'll tell her you said so too."

I bit back a sigh and stared up at the ceiling. "Don't suppose you'll reconsider telling me where to find her?"

"Definitely not, but you get points for asking," Jana said cheerily.

We ended the call, and I stood up from the couch. Restless, I paced in front of the windows. I was a doer. I liked to have a plan and put it into motion. That helped me a lot when I was playing ball. Right now, all it did was make me feel helpless.

"So?" Belle asked.

I turned to her with a shrug. "Jana's got the thing with the other attorney handled. Zoe's at her parents' but Jana won't tell me where that is."

Tristan glanced up, his shrewd gaze scanning my face. "Belle's right," he said flatly.

Belle grinned and then looked to him. "About what?" she asked, saving me from the same question.

Tristan kept his gaze on me. "You're in love.""

Coming from him, it didn't have the frilly excitement of Belle's earlier declaration. As such, it hit me hard—a bolt to my heart. I stared at Tristan. My breath lodged like a fist in my throat, jumpstarting with the next thud of my heart.

I looked across the kitchen table at my mother. Her auburn hair was pulled back into a tidy twist, the silvery streaks in it standing out against its brightness. She sipped her coffee and flipped through the newspaper. After a fortifying sip of my coffee, I took a breath and eyed her.

"Mom, I need your opinion."

She folded the paper and looked over at me. "On what?"

I'd arrived two nights ago, and my parents had taken it in stride. I visited every few months as it was. I didn't usually show up on short notice, but they were gracious enough not to badger me. When it came to parents, I'd drawn a good hand in life. Beyond the fact they'd both been workaholics—I came by that trait honestly—they were involved, caring parents. Work had been such a focus for them, parenting was a bit of a second thought, but they'd distractedly done their loving best. I also felt lucky to have parents who actually liked each other. Their tendency to not focus overly on me had been a blessing when I showed up the other night. I knew they sensed something was afoot with me, but they didn't press.

Another deep breath. "I got involved with one of my clients. I referred his case, but now a few things have made me think maybe I should, I don't know... Ugh." I paused to take a gulp of coffee. That was the crux of my problem. I had no easy way to clear the air. I worked for myself. I might've waited a bit longer than I should, but I had transferred Ethan's case. I just felt mortified about it and didn't like having it hanging over me.

I looked over at my mother who looked, well, surprised. But not upset or horrified like I'd feared. When I didn't say anything else because I had no idea what to say, she spoke.

"So that's what got you all bothered. If you referred the case to someone else, I'm not sure what you're worried about now," she said quietly. My mother was ever practical and never prone to drama.

I traced the mug handle with my fingertip. "Well, it's just not the kind of thing I do. I never imagined I'd let something like that happen, so..."

I didn't want to get into the thing with Ted Duncan with her. All in all, it wasn't the core of what was eating at me.

"No, it's not the kind of thing you do, but then you don't really date. At all. Are you still seeing him? Well, I suppose I shouldn't assume it's a him," she said with a slight smile.

"It's a him," I muttered. "Am I that bad you weren't even sure if I was into guys?"

She lifted one shoulder in a slow shrug. "Not that it matters, but you've never brought anyone home. I didn't think much of it because you threw yourself into work. You're so much like your father and I about that. I have worried that you weren't making time for a personal life. While we both worked a lot, we worked together, so it was something we shared. And we had you. Of course, we dragged you to the office with us, so it's entirely our fault you followed in our footsteps. But that isn't my point. My point is I've hoped you'd eventually find someone. Tell me about him. I'd guess he means a lot to you, or you certainly wouldn't have gotten involved with him, seeing as he was your client at the start."

I don't know what it was about how she said that, but it hit me hard—a jolt right to my solar plexus. My heart clenched, and I swallowed against the sudden rush of emotion. My mother had zeroed in on the thing that was making my heart ache. I missed Ethan like crazy. I'd dashed out of my office for no good reason other than feeling overwhelmed with it all. Between Sarah's practical advice and now my mother's, it was painfully clear that no matter how much I wanted a way to clear things up over my lapse in professional judgment, I'd done the only thing I could do and sent Ethan's case onward to another attorney. The muddle I was in now was all of my own making.

My mother cleared her throat, and I realized she was waiting. On the heels of another deep breath, I continued, "I guess he does. I'm not really sure what to do about that. He's not a regular kind of guy."

She cocked her head to the side and circled her hand. "Do tell."

"His name is Ethan Walsh. He's..."

She cut in. "From the Seattle Stars?"

At my nod, she grinned. "Your father is a fan."

"Since when did Dad start watching soccer?" I asked, stunned.

"Since the Seattle Stars went big time. Now that he's not working all the time, he enjoys a number of things. He's going to be so excited!"

"Mom, could you calm down? I don't even know what's happening with Ethan yet. Let's not start the 'meet the family' plans yet."

Her grin morphed into a soft smile. She reached over and squeezed my hand. "Of course. But based on the look on your face, I'd say he means a lot to you. What are you doing hiding out here? Get back to Seattle and see him."

———

The remainder of my morning and afternoon passed quietly. My mother left to run errands, and I helped my father rearrange the furniture in his office. By the time evening rolled around, I was antsy to get back to Seattle. I can't say I'd come to a conclusion on anything, but I missed Ethan and was feeling like I was stalling over nothing. I hopped back in my car and figured I could make it home in time to see him that night.

Roughly two hours later, water slapped against my car where it sat on the side of the road, halfway in a ditch. I looked out through the blurry windows and beat back the threat of tears. My hope to get home quickly had been thwarted by the heavy rain. It had gone from a soft drizzle to a steady pour. I'd hit a puddle and slid sideways off the road. My car skidded just far enough into the ditch that I wouldn't be getting out without some help.

"Shit, shit, shit," I muttered, wearily thumping my fist on the defenseless steering wheel. My options for getting help were to call a tow truck, or Jana. My parents were a good two hours behind me now, and I didn't want to ask them to trek this far to help me.

I pulled my phone out, only to see another few texts from Ethan. His last one made me burst into tears.

Come on, Zoe. Now I'm not just bugging you. I'm worried. Jana won't tell me how to find you. Please call me.

I took a shuddering breath and managed to stop crying. Emotionally, I was whipsawing all over the place. One minute, I wanted to forget all about Ethan and go back to my tidy, professional, boring life. The next, I ached to see him. Without thinking, I hit the call button on his text. He answered instantly.

"Bloody hell, Zoe. You're scaring the shite out of me. When are you coming back?"

His greeting came flying at me, and I burst into tears all over again.

"Hey Zo, okay, okay. Calm down. I didn't mean to sound all mad. It's just you haven't..."

"It's okay, I'm..." I paused on a hiccup and to try to catch my breath. I felt like a blithering idiot, a feeling I wasn't particularly familiar with.

"Where are you?" he asked, his tone softer.

"On the side of the road."

"Come again."

I took a breath and haltingly explained where I was.

"Right then, I'll come get you. Belle will want to come, and I don't know if I can hold her off. Will you mind?"

I started laughing. It was either that, or I'd start crying again.

Ethan waited quietly until I managed to stop laughing.

"It's fine if Belle comes, but you'd better let her know I'm not usually a mess like this."

"You're never a mess," he said, his tone soft and laced with something I didn't know how to interpret. It made my heart clench.

Chapter Twenty-Seven

ETHAN

The drive through the rainy night felt like forever even though it was only about an hour. Belle was chatty, as she always was. She insisted we bring Tristan along too.

"Because it'll be weird if it's just me. I'm your sister, and you've never brought a woman to meet any of us. This is big, Ethan," Belle explained as I drove.

I had warned Zoe that Belle would want to come, but I hadn't been thinking about how Belle might treat this. Since she'd declared I was in love, she couldn't wait to meet Zoe. I was a bit relieved she'd wanted Tristan to come because he was a modulating influence on anyone. He knew all of my sisters pretty well and would keep Belle in check. Or so I hoped. Zoe didn't sound well when we talked. She was always together, so I didn't quite know what to do about her crying. Having four sisters meant I had some experience with crying, so it didn't rattle me the way it did some blokes. I just hadn't counted on my heart viscerally aching with concern over Zoe though.

I kept on driving while Belle chattered. In an effort to

get my mind off of worrying about Zoe, I looped back to a conversation I'd attempted to start earlier with Belle.

"I know you'll talk about my alleged love life all night, but how about a bit more detail on why you're here? You're always welcome, but usually you call," I said, glancing in the rear view mirror. I caught Tristan's grin out of the corner of my eye. He was up front since his legs were too long for him to be comfortable in the back seat.

Belle caught my eyes in the mirror before looking away. In the two days she'd been here, she'd mostly camped out at our flat, but she'd also dashed off for coffee this morning and came back seeming out of sorts. I fixed my gaze on the rainy highway in front of me, the rain illuminated in the head-lights as I drove along. After a moment of quiet, Belle sighed heavily. She muttered something to herself.

"Come again?" I prompted.

"I'm here to see someone," she finally said.

"Someone?"

"Uh huh."

Finally. I had something to wonder about other than Zoe. "Who? And why don't I know anything about this until now?"

"Oh my God. Don't get all big brother on me."

"Don't show up out of nowhere then," I returned. "Who are you here to see?"

She mumbled again, leading Tristan to laugh under his breath.

Belle swatted Tristan on the shoulder. "Oh stuff it. Fine. I'm here to see Mack."

"Mack? Mack Dawson?"

Mack was a player on the Seattle Stars, one of the Americans who also happened to be from Seattle, so he was a local favorite. He was an offensive player and bloody good. I liked the guy. He was easy-going and funny. Right now though, I suddenly didn't like him.

"What the hell is he doing getting involved with you

without me knowing about it?" I asked her, flicking my eyes to the mirror again, only to see Belle studiously staring out the side window.

Tristan caught my eyes as I looked forward again and gave his head a little shake. I doubted he knew more than me, but seeing as I'd been irritable and distracted ever since Belle had been here, he probably had noticed more of how she was doing.

Belle surprised me by answering. "He didn't even know I was here until this morning, so don't go thinking he was doing something behind your back."

I had no fucking clue what to say to that. I was saved from this out of the blue conversation when Tristan gestured ahead. I looked to the side of the road ahead and saw a car halfway in the ditch off the highway. I didn't actually know what kind of car Zoe drove, seeing as we'd walked just about everywhere we needed to go thus far. Tristan, of course, had made me ask Zoe for the GPS coordinates for where she was based on her phone maps. I should've known he'd have his phone out monitoring as we drove through the dark, rainy night. We'd exited off I-5 onto this smaller highway roughly a half hour ago. It was darker and narrower, and I didn't like thinking about Zoe sitting in her car alone in the rain.

I pulled up behind what I hoped like hell was Zoe's car and climbed out quickly, instantly getting soaked by a passing car and the splash from its tires. I jogged to the driver's side door and knocked on the window, relieved to see Zoe there. The dim light from the car's interior light cast a soft glow on her through the blurry view. My heart clenched tightly and then set to pounding hard and fast.

The last two days had been bloody hell for me. I was far past worrying about what it meant that I was in so deep. At the dim click of the door unlocking, I yanked it open and leaned inside. I meant to say something—hell if I know what. The second I saw her eyes and the intensity of feeling reflected there, I slid my hand into her hair and kissed her.

She gasped and then tugged me closer, sliding her hand up around my neck. I didn't care that I was getting soaked, didn't care that this was the most awkward angle ever—what with me leaning into her car and almost falling into her— didn't care that we were on the side of the highway with my sister and Tristan as our personal audience, all I cared about was Zoe wasn't out of reach anymore. She was living, breathing here, and mine.

I tore my lips from hers and dusted kisses all over her face, murmuring how much I'd missed her and so on. Somewhere in there, I murmured, "I love you."

It came out so easily, so naturally, that it didn't give me pause. Zoe went still and drew back slightly, her eyes wide and luminous.

"What did you say?" she asked, her voice low and breathy.

I could feel her pulse fluttering wildly under my thumb brushing along the soft skin of her neck. Awareness hit me, and I went as still as she did. Uncertainty flashed through me. I had no fucking clue if she felt anything close to the way I did. For a moment, I wondered if I'd gone and lost my bloody mind. Then, a sense of certainty followed. I meant what I said, so there was no sense in equivocating.

"I said I love you."

She kept staring at me, so long I started to wonder if I'd just gone and made the biggest fool of myself. Then, her hand slid down from my neck, coming to rest over my heart.

"I got a little freaked out. I don't usually bolt like that," she said.

I managed a nod because what the hell else was I supposed to do? In all my years, I'd always had the grace of the upper hand when it came to women. I'd never thought of it like that, but in this moment, I knew it to be true. I'd never been the one to hand my heart over like this. Because no one had ever, ever meant as much to me as Zoe did. Right here, right now, while I waited in the rain on the side of the road, she held my heart in her hands whether she knew it or not.

All of the sudden, her eyes teared up, and she said something, but I couldn't hear between the rain, the cars driving by and her crying.

"Luv, come again?"

Her eyes slammed to mine again. "I said I love you!"

Well then. Bloody hell. All was right with the world.

I dipped my head and kissed her again.

Just then, someone nudged my back. I straightened to find Tristan standing there.

"If you don't get back to the car, Belle will be sharing this moment with you," he said with a wry grin. "Only reason she's not here yet is it's bloody awful out and she forgot her raincoat."

Zoe leaned around my shoulder. "Hey Tristan, thanks for coming to get me with Ethan."

He nodded, ever polite. "Of course. Give me a few, and I think we can get your car out of the ditch. Why don't you two take your car, and I'll follow with Belle?"

I thanked the stars for Tristan. He was ever practical and always planning ahead. If he thought we could deal with Zoe's car, we likely could.

———

Not much later, I was driving north with Zoe sitting beside me. Belle had reluctantly agreed to ride back with Tristan in my car. I think the only reason she agreed was she could see I wanted to be alone with Zoe. She'd also gotten to chat with Zoe in my car while Tristan and I dealt with getting Zoe's car out of the ditch. It wasn't too hard. I volunteered to stay out in the rain and push it since I'd already gotten good and drenched.

Zoe's car was a compact something or other. I'd volunteered to drive, seeing as she looked weary, and I knew she'd already been driving for a few hours in the rain. Her easy agreement to that let me know how tired she was. I had my hand on her thigh because it was physically impossible for me not to touch her. Mere inches separated us between the seats, and it felt like way too much distance.

The relief I felt at being back beside her was a bit much and had I been in my right mind, it would have bothered me. But it was Zoe and I hadn't been sane ever since the first time I kissed her, so it didn't bother me in the slightest. The only problem was the fact I was driving distracted with my cock so hard I had to keep shifting in my seat. I'd missed her and everything felt raw. Somehow being soaked from the rain added to the overall feeling.

I glanced over, and my breath caught. She was so fucking beautiful. The headlights of passing cars illuminated her rich auburn hair. Her hair was damp and drying in wild waves around her shoulders. I felt myself drifting deeper into the need pounding through me. I needed to get some kind of grip, so I latched onto conversation.

"I hope Belle didn't badger you while we were getting your car dealt with," I commented.

Zoe looked to me, flashing a small smile. "Oh no. She was quite nice. I'm glad I got to meet her. She went on about what a great brother you are."

I chuckled. Of course Belle would do that.

"Eh, did she then? Well, don't listen to everything she says about me, especially any pranks I played on her when we were wee ones."

Zoe laughed softly and curled her hand over mine where it rested on her thigh to give it a squeeze. A wave of need slammed into me. I glanced to her, catching her eyes briefly. That only made it worse. Fuck me. I wasn't up for waiting this forever drive. I'd already told Belle I'd be home in the morning. When she'd tried to say Zoe should come to my flat, Tristan had shut her up with one glance.

I eyed an exit off the highway ahead and took it. Within

seconds, we were on an unfamiliar side road in the rainy darkness.

"Where are you going?" Zoe asked, her voice breathy in the quiet space of her car.

"Here," I said the moment I saw a sign for a park.

I'd come to learn Washington State loved parks. They were all over the place. I kept my hand on the cool skin of Zoe's thigh and steered down a short road that ended in a parking lot—a completely deserted parking lot encircled by trees. I came to an abrupt stop and turned to her.

Whatever she'd been thinking, she appeared to have tuned into my channel. Her eyes flashed with desire in the soft illumination cast from the single light in the corner of the small parking area. I didn't feel much like talking. I slid my hand between her knees, reminded yet again that I bloody loved her penchant for skirts. Even on this cool rainy evening, she had a skirt on, one of her usual proper skirts. Perfect for me to shove up out of the way and slide a finger over the silk at the apex of her thighs.

It was hot and wet. At her gasp, I tugged her to me. It was messy and not the least bit smooth, but she ended up sitting astride me and laughing softly. Once the upheaval of getting her into my lap was over, I looked up at her. Our eyes caught, and she went quiet. She settled down on me, and I could feel her damp heat against my cock through my jeans.

My heart felt as if it might explode, but it felt so good to be here with her, I didn't worry about it. The air around us felt hot, electric and weighted with a depth of feeling I'd never experienced. I sucked in a breath and dipped my head to taste her. Her skin was salty and sweet with a hint of the cool rain outside. I made my way up her neck with kisses, licks and nips. The second our lips met, any semblance of control I had was lost. I poured everything I felt into our kiss—days of longing and need, of missing her, and of not really knowing what to do with how I felt.

It was hot, messy, and wild. She rolled her hips against

me, little moans and gasps coming from her into my mouth, until I thought I would explode if I couldn't be inside of her. I reached between us and shoved her panties out of the way. Her slick folds were soaked. I sank two fingers into her at once, groaning when she tore her lips from mine and cried out. In a fumble, she reached between us and yanked at the buttons of my jeans. I wanted to savor this, but I needed her too fiercely.

My need for her was raw and unrelenting, ferocious in its depth. In seconds, she freed my cock, pushing my briefs out of the way. She stroked once, but I couldn't wait and reached between us, lifting her hips with one hand and positioning my cock at her entrance with the other. Her wet heat kissed my cock, and I glanced up, needing to see her.

She shifted impatiently.

"Zoe," I murmured. It was a bloody miracle I managed to speak over the rushed beat of my heart and the need coursing through me.

She opened her eyes and met mine. I held still, though it took every last ounce of discipline I had.

Everything narrowed to this moment. With nothing but the sound of the rain falling outside and drumming on the roof of the car, it was as if we were alone in the universe. My heart thudded and need lashed at me, but I held still.

"I meant what I said."

She bit her lip and angled her head to the side. "What?"

"I love you."

She took a shuddering breath before nodding. "Me too."

The frayed thread I'd been hanging onto snapped. I arched my hips and brought her down at once, surging into her. She cried out, her head falling forward to bring her forehead to mine. With our breath mingling, we started rocking into each other. Her channel pulsed around me—a wet, velvet clench made to drive me mad.

It wasn't smooth. It was rough, hot, wet, and messy. Inside of a few seconds, she was crying out, her core throbbing around me. My release came as a sharp lash of pleasure, whipsawing through me. I spent myself inside of her and leaned my head back when hers fell to my shoulder. I held her close against me and simply breathed her in, absorbing the scent and feel of her. We ungracefully untangled ourselves after we caught our breath.

A bit later, I came out of the bathroom at Zoe's flat, warm and dry after a steamy hot shower. She was standing in the kitchen and turned to face me with two mugs in hand.

"Hot chocolate," she announced before herding me onto the couch.

We watched something on the telly. I have no idea what, but it involved Zoe's legs hooked over my lap, so all was good. I fell asleep with her warm against me and finally able to relax for the first time in days.

EPILOGUE - ZOE

I stood in the hallway at the stadium, listening to the distant sounds of the crowd filtering out gradually. The Stars had won tonight. This was only my second season of watching them play regularly, and it was a bit bumpier than last year. They had two injured starters and the backups couldn't quite make up the difference. As it was, they hadn't been expected to win tonight. Ethan had played a stellar game, but then I was of the opinion he always did.

I heard his voice teasing Liam about something. A smile bloomed from my heart straight to my toes. It was that bad. I kept thinking the thrill would wear off with him, but it hadn't yet.

He rounded the corner and grinned when he saw me. I still thought he was too handsome for me. I mean, my God, it was ridiculous. He walked with that easy swagger that he didn't even realize was a swagger. Women still swooned just looking at him. He reached me and swept me up in his arms.

I laughed and glanced down. It was silly for him to pick me up, seeing as I was almost as tall as him, but he did it anyway. I met his teasing green gaze, the one I'd used to think insouciant, but now all it did was make me wet.

"Nice game," I murmured as he threaded a hand in my hair and pulled me close.

"Mmm. What do I get for it?" he replied with his lips moving against mine.

He didn't give me a chance to answer and proceeded to kiss me senseless right there in front of everyone walking by.

EPILOGUE - ETHAN

Zoe stood by the railing, her hair blowing in a swirl from the wind, and looked out over the ocean. She'd insisted I needed to visit the islands in Puget Sound, so we were headed out to San Juan Island for a long weekend at an inn. I had a bloody perfect plan to propose, but I was suddenly impatient. Against the slightly overcast sky, her hair was so bright and she was so fucking beautiful, I threw my plan into the wind.

I crossed the boat and leaned against the railing beside her, slipping my arm about her waist and tugging her tight against me. She glanced my way, a lock of hair blowing across her eyes. I reached up to brush it out of the way.

"It's lovely," I said.

"I don't think lovely quite cuts it," she said with a grin.

She was right. The air was scented crisp and salty from the ocean. Seattle receded behind us, its skyline distant as the boat kept moving away. Gulls called and swooped. We'd seen a pod of orcas only moments before. I was definitely out of my element, but I didn't mind. As long as Zoe was with me, I didn't give a bloody damn where I was.

"Perhaps not. That's not what I came to say though."

"Oh? Did you learn how to drive the boat yet?" she asked with a sly grin.

I'd ventured to chat with the boat captain and announced to Zoe I thought we'd paid way too much for a drive over the water, but I didn't care to tease about that now.

"Luv, let's get married."

Her eyes widened and then she started laughing. After a beat, tears were sliding down her cheeks. I tugged her into me, turning my back against the railing and pulling her flush against me. I brushed her hair back.

"I had it all planned, but I didn't want to wait," I murmured as I dusted kisses over her cheeks. "I didn't mean to make you cry."

She dragged the corner of her sleeve across her cheeks, interrupting me as I kissed my way to her lips.

"They're good tears," she said with a hiccup. "What do you mean you had it all planned?"

I leaned back, soaking her in. "I meant to wait until tonight at dinner. I have a ring and all."

She stared at me, and another tear slipped down her cheek. "Oh. Oh wow. So you really are asking me to marry you."

I nodded, wondering if I'd stepped wrong here. It had been roughly a year since that rainy night when I'd finally faced the fact I loved her. In the intervening time, we'd moved in together and were presently in the midst of trying to find a house outside of the bustle of downtown Seattle. She'd weathered the kerfuffle over our relationship becoming public news. As she'd worried, there'd been a few public comments that she'd met me because she'd been hired to handle my legal case. To my relief, several colleagues of hers had publicly noted she'd done precisely as required and referred my case onward. I was still annoyed over that bit because I'd thought it entirely pointless. But, the dust had settled and for that I was relieved. Zoe was a worrier and ridiculously particular. Every so often, it occurred to me I should be thankful she'd broken a few rules for me.

Once again, I wasn't following the plan and even though it wasn't her who'd done the planning, I bet it bothered her. That thought made me grin.

She eyed me, a slow smile spreading. "What?"

"Just thinking it's a better plan with you not to have a plan," I offered, threading my hand into her hair and pulling her close.

"So, what do you say?" I murmured.

"Yes. Of course, I say yes," she replied, her cheeks flushing pink. "You can't think I'd say anything else."

In a flash, the weight of the moment hit me. I knew well Zoe held my heart in her hands, but my tendency to be confident let me forget to worry about what that meant.

I leaned back and gulped in air. "No luv. It's not quite that simple. I still can't quite believe you haven't run me out. Lest you think I have the upper hand, never forget that it's the opposite. I'd do anything for you."

Another tear rolled down her cheek, and then I was kissing her with clouds scudding across the sky and the ocean breeze swirling around us.

———

Thank you for reading Out Of Bounds - I hope you loved Ethan & Zoe's story!

For more steamy, sports romance, Tristan & Daisy's story is up next in Play Me. This is a scorching hot friends to lovers story. "...this author blows it out of the water and comes up with another story that makes me think and go...WOW...BLOODY AMAZING....WOW." Don't miss Tristan's story!

Keep reading for a sneak peek!

Be sure to sign up for my newsletter for the latest news,
teasers & more! Click here to sign up: http://
jhcroixauthor.com/subscribe/

EXCERPT: PLAY ME BY J.H. CROIX; ALL RIGHTS RESERVED

Tristan

I rounded a corner, heading down the hallway to my office, and collided with a woman walking so fast, she nearly knocked me over. Her blonde hair flew in my face, and she caught her balance by grabbing onto my arm.

"Oh my God! I'm so... Ack!"

The woman exclaimed as her feet scrambled and, hell if I know how, she managed to drag us both to the floor in her tumble. It was then my body discovered that this woman was a veritable buffet of curves. I could feel her full breasts pressing against my chest and, as luck would have it, my cock was nestled at the apex of her luscious thighs. She was soft and tempting all over. I still had no fucking clue who she was, but my body would've been happy to stay right where I was.

Small problem—she was wiggling out from under me inside of a second. "Oh my God! I can't believe that just happened."

Her voice sounded familiar, but I couldn't place it.

I had some manners, so I rolled to the side and pushed myself up. I glanced down to see her brushing her blonde hair away from her face and looking up at me. My heart nearly cracked a rib with its swift kick.

Daisy Knight sat on the hallway floor before me. Bloody hell, she was gorgeous. The last time I'd seen her had been almost a year ago. We had what I'd chalked up to an almost one-night stand, and I'd yet to forget it. We hadn't even gotten close to the full act, and she'd still left me more tied up than any woman—ever. I'd hoped to see her again. Yet, whether by accident or design, Daisy managed to avoid me so completely ever since then I figured that was her preference. Given that her two best friends were married to two of my best mates, I didn't doubt she'd gone out of her way to avoid seeing me. I had plenty of other things to focus on and eschewed attachments, so I'd figured I'd never get the chance to find out how amazing sex with her could have been.

Daisy's wide brown eyes met mine. With the feel of her body imprinted against mine and staring down at her, my cock twitched. Her lips parted—her plump lips with her slightly lopsided smile. I could see the rise and fall of her breasts with her breath. It didn't fucking help matters that she was wearing a blouse that pulled tightly across them. My eyes dipped into the valley between them. My cock hardened, and I dragged my eyes up. Right. We were in the hallway in the medical research wing of the hospital. It wouldn't do to have me leering at her.

I held a hand out. "Hello, Daisy. Long time, no see," I said, keeping my tone level.

She gripped my hand, and I helped her up. Once she was standing, she brushed her hands over her skirt and adjusted her blouse. None of that made me forget any inch of her delectable body. But I had manners and needed to respect the distance she seemed to want to keep from me. I took a step back.

"What brings you here?" I finally asked.

Her cheeks were slightly pink. Between the heavy fall of

her blonde hair, those wide doe eyes, and her porcelain skin, the subtle flush nearly did me in.

She straightened her shoulders. "Hello Tristan. It has been a while, hasn't it?"

I nodded and considered whether it was worth mentioning the last time I saw her. Likely not, so I stayed quiet.

"Actually, I'm here to see Dr. Wells. He's temporarily covering the clinic for one of the studies I manage," she explained. "They told me his office was down here, but nothing's marked, so I lost track. What are you doing here?"

My heart gave another kick to my ribs. Daisy had known I'd graduated from medical school. She also had to know I'd been sidelined from playing ball after a brutal injury to my left knee at the end of last season and wouldn't be back to play for another few months. Most of my life had been playing football, otherwise known as soccer here in the United States. I'd signed with the Seattle Stars a few seasons back, along with several mates from England. All through university and through my professional career, I'd kept on track and finished my medical degree. It had been loads of work, but I'd known I wanted something other than sports for my career because it wouldn't last forever.

For now though, I was temporarily running the research clinic within the hospital while the director was traveling, a clinic that happened to have signed onto a study for a new medication trial before I took over. It was ideal for me because I didn't want a long-term position, just something to fill the next few months until I could start playing ball again. I should've connected the dots and realized they led straight back to Daisy. She appeared to have completely forgotten my last name.

I was about to answer when the flush on her cheeks deepened. "Tristan Wells. Right. I should've figured that one out. I bet you think I'm a dolt," she said with a wry laugh. "I didn't forget your name, it's just I've never called you Dr. Wells, so it didn't sink in."

"No one would ever accuse you of being a dolt," I replied. "Follow me."

I resumed walking toward my office, and she turned to follow beside me. I had a stern little convo with my cock on the walk down that hallway. Fortunately, it was a fair distance because my body's response to being near Daisy was off the charts. This woman just did it for me. She turned every invisible knob on the dials of my desire. I'd kept women in a tidy compartment in my life. I might have access to plenty, what with my college and then pro years as a soccer star, but I considered relationships messy. I loved sex as much as any man, and I found it pretty easy to keep it to nothing more than that.

I stepped through my office door and gestured for Daisy to enter first. Her generous hips swayed with each step. As usual, she somehow managed to pull off this entirely professional way of dressing that had a hint of naughty to it. I knew how wild her response to me had been, so it only amped up my reaction to her. She wore a fitted skirt, a tad bit shorter and tighter than the usual professional skirt, that rested just above her knees paired with black kitten heeled shoes. Atop that she had on a fitted blouse. Perfectly respectable at a glance unless you happened to notice her breasts strained the buttons. She walked to the windows and looked out before spinning to face me. With her thick blonde hair, her heart shaped face and those brown doe eyes, bloody fucking hell I wanted her.

I'd somehow managed to forget just how tempting she was. I reminded myself rather forcefully why Daisy was here. Work. Nothing more. Just because I wanted to bend her over my desk didn't mean it would be happening.

"So you're here to check in on the study protocol, I suppose?" I asked as I rounded my desk. Before sitting down, I gestured for her to take the seat across from me. Once she was seated, I sat down and leaned back.

She opened her purse and pulled out a pair of glasses. Fuck me. I'd never seen her in glasses. This would not help. Oblivious to my internal state, she perched them on her nose and pulled out a small computer tablet. She tapped a few times and then glanced up.

"That's exactly why I'm here. When Dr. Horton signed the clinic on to our study, we were in the planning stages then. Since he left, there wasn't much to deal with, but now we're ready to start coordinating with you on patients who choose to enroll in the trial. This here," she paused and faced the tablet screen toward me. "Shows the process for how we'll track patients in our system. Since you've been here...?"

Her words trailed off with a questioning look.

"A few months," I added for her.

"Oh, then you must be familiar with this for the other study with our program."

"I am. It's very straightforward. The tech team here has already set up the online linkage for our unit, so there should be no issues."

Daisy closed the tablet and slipped the tablet back into her rather voluminous purse before looking back to me. "Excellent."

A moment of silence fell, the air instantly feeling electric. What the hell was it with how she affected me? I'd better get a handle on it because as far as I knew, I'd be working with her regularly now.

She idly twirled a lock of hair around her finger and eyed me as if she was considering something. "So, how are you?" she asked brightly.

I shrugged. "I'm well. Yourself?"

She worried her bottom lip for a moment, sending a shot of lust straight through me again. "Same, same. I'd imagine this last year might've been hard since you were out with your knee injury."

Ah, so I hadn't fallen off the face of the earth in her mind. "It wasn't great as far as that went, but I'll be back in play next season. Meanwhile, I'm here."

She kept twirling that lock of hair around her finger and eyed me. "I hope you didn't think I was avoiding you," she said abruptly.

If I'd been wondering, now I knew for certain. Daisy was many things, but she wasn't one to shy away from something. Unless it bothered her.

For a beat, I considered politely going along with her. But I didn't quite feel like it. Rather, I wanted to push her.

I stood, my chair rolling back behind me, the sound of its wheels loud in the quiet office. Rounding the desk, I leaned my hips against it and looked down at her.

"I think you were."

Her gorgeous brown eyes widened, and she stood quickly. Oh bloody perfect. I'd pissed her off. Precisely what I wanted.

She was mere inches from me. I couldn't have planned it better. She rested her hands on her hips and glared at me. "I was not!"

I curled my hands on the edge of the desk, solely because if I didn't I'd be yanking her to me inside of a second and that wouldn't do. Daisy and I had nearly set each other on fire with a few kisses and heavy petting. For reasons unknown to me she'd put the brakes on hard and literally dashed away from me. Yet, I wanted to draw this out for the sake of seeing where it went.

I met her flashing eyes and arched a brow. "Really? You mean to tell me that in almost a year, you somehow managed to avoid every single time I happened to be with my mates? I find that nearly impossible. I used to see you every few weeks. We were about the let things go somewhere, and I haven't seen you since. What I want to know is why you're so tied up about it? Weren't you the one who said it was nothing?"

I was taunting her and I damn well knew it. Distantly, I wondered if I'd gone mad, but I didn't quite care to contemplate that just now.

Her cheeks flushed a deep pink, and she pointed at me. "I am *not* tied up about it."

Then, she actually jabbed me in the chest with her finger.

———

DAISY

I knew I was flustered, and I knew I needed to get a grip, but I couldn't think straight. I jabbed Tristan's chest with my index finger and repeated myself. I hated when people repeated themselves, and here I was doing exactly that.

"I am *not* tied up about it."

Tristan looked down at me for a beat. Sweet hell. He was too handsome for words. He was tall, dark and mysterious and so sexy it was dangerous. At least for my health and well-being. His black curls were slightly rumpled. His hazel eyes locked with mine, and my breath lodged in my throat. Heat spread like wildfire in my veins.

This was not supposed to be happening. About a year ago, I'd had a few too many glasses of wine, and I'd given in to the thrumming need Tristan had elicited inside of me ever since I'd known him. I'd meant for it to be nothing more than sex. I'd figured Tristan would let me down like every guy did. Problem was, once his mouth was on mine and his hands were mapping my body, I came close to two things I'd been chasing forever—an orgasm and intimacy. Completely clothed with his mouth driving me mad and sweet streaks of pleasure shooting through me, I'd felt as if we were caught in a web together. I was so accustomed to sex being distant and mechanical—to thinking too much.

With every fiber of me desperately wanting to let go into the best feeling ever, I'd shoved him away from me and dashed away. Because all of it scared me. I knew perfectly well how Tristan viewed relationships. According to my two best friends who happened to be respectively paired up with his buddies from the Seattle Stars, he deemed them messy, and he didn't do messy.

So there I was nearly gaga over a guy who I just couldn't expect anything from. Little did he know I wanted nothing more than to settle down. I couldn't make a fool of myself over him. Leave it to me to be stuck alone pining for a man I couldn't have.

Tristan arched a brow. Hell, he even had an amazing face. Strong features with a blade of a nose, and a permanent five o'clock shadow. I remembered just how his stubble felt against my skin. As these thoughts tumbled through my mind, my pulse took off at a gallop and I could hardly breathe.

He curled his hand around mine where my finger pressed into his chest. My belly did a slow flip and everything in me tightened with need. He was quiet, his eyes boring into mine. I felt prickly hot all over, exposed and vulnerable. On the heels of this came anger. It infuriated me that I wanted him so much.

"I think you are," he said, his low voice sending a hot shiver down my spine. "What I want to know is why?"

My cheeks were hot, and I willed the heat away, an entirely futile endeavor. I wanted to shake my head wildly and to argue with him, but I didn't. My ability to speak deserted me the second he lifted his hand and traced it along my hairline, slowly sliding his fingers through my hair.

My breath came in short pants, while my pulse lunged. Need throbbed at my core. I wanted him so much. This was precisely why I'd avoided him. I knew how it felt to have him touch me, and it was dangerously good.

"If you're not lying, then have dinner with me," he said, his eyes never once breaking from mine.

Sheer stubbornness kept me from closing my eyes. I wanted to, but dammit, he was not going to see how much he rattled me.

"Fine. Let's have dinner," I snapped.

He still had my hand caught in his, while he idly sifted through my hair with his other hand. Heat was rolling through me and my low belly clenched, but I would not let myself push him away. I could handle this. I'd show him he didn't have the upper hand, and I'd get over my body's obsession with him.

His mouth curled at one corner. Oh fuck. God, he was too much for any woman to deal with and not lose her mind. "Tonight then?" he asked.

I didn't want to do this tonight. I needed time to armor myself. But if I said no, I'd look like I was chickening out. I couldn't do that, so I nodded and willed myself not to moan at the feel of his fingers brushing against the skin of my neck as they slid through my hair.

When I nodded, his eyes widened slightly. Good. He'd expected me to put him off. Hell no. I could handle this. It would be good. I needed to get past the awkwardness I felt and stop avoiding him.

He released my hand. I stepped back, maybe more quickly than I should have, but I needed to get some distance between us. His eyes took on a gleam and instantly I knew he'd noticed. I lifted my chin. "Where and when?" I asked, my tone coming out bitchy. I didn't care. I needed my inner bitch loud and proud right now.

"I'll pick you up. Six o'clock."

I so didn't want him to pick me up, but if I argued about that, it would seem silly.

"Fine. Don't be cheap," I said as I turned to spin away.

His low chuckle followed me to the door. I was about to step through it when he spoke.

"Daisy?"

I glanced back to him.

"We *will* finish what we started before."

My cheeks flamed hot again, but I clung to my dignity with my fingertips. "You don't call the shots," I retorted.

He shrugged. "Maybe not, but I know you want it as much as I do."

I had no words for that. He had no idea how right he was.

———

Available Now!

Play Me

Go here to sign up for information on new releases & get a FREE copy of one of my books! http://jhcroixauthor.com/subscribe/

FIND MY BOOKS

Thank you for reading Out Of Bounds! I hope you enjoyed the story. If so, you can help other readers find my books in a variety of ways.

1) Write a review!
2) Sign up for my newsletter, so you can receive information about upcoming new releases & receive a FREE copy of one of my books: http://jhcroixauthor.com/subscribe/
3) Like and follow my Amazon Author page at https://amazon.com/author/jhcroix
4) Follow me on Bookbub at https://www.bookbub.com/authors/j-h-croix
5) Follow me on Instagram https://www.instagram.com/jhcroix/
6) Like my Facebook page at https://www.facebook.com/jhcroix

———

Brit Boys Sports Romance

The Play
Big Win
Out Of Bounds
Play Me
Naughty Wish
Swoon Series
This Crazy Love
Wait For Me
Break My Fall
Truly Madly Mine
Into The Fire Series
Burn For Me
Slow Burn
Burn So Bad
Hot Mess
Burn So Good
Sweet Fire
Play With Fire
Melt With You
Burn For You
Crash & Burn
Diamond Creek Alaska Novels
When Love Comes
Follow Love
Love Unbroken
Love Untamed
Tumble Into Love
Christmas Nights
Last Frontier Lodge Novels
Christmas on the Last Frontier
Love at Last
Just This Once
Falling Fast
Stay With Me
When We Fall
Hold Me Close

Crazy For You
Just Us
Catamount Lion Shifters
Protected Mate
Chosen Mate
Fated Mate
Destined Mate
A Catamount Christmas
The Lion Within
Lion Lost & Found

ACKNOWLEDGMENTS

Hugs, kisses and thanks to my hubby for cheering my dreams on. I wrote this book during a particularly busy and challenging time, and his support never wavered. A bow of thanks to Yoly Cortez from Cormar Covers for her patience with me and for creating yet another amazing cover. The words *thank you* don't encompass how much my readers mean to me, but it's what we have, so **thank you** from the bottom of my heart. Your emails, messages & more mean the world to me. Special thanks to Beth P., Terri E. & Janine for being my proofreader angels!

xoxo

J.H. Croix

ABOUT THE AUTHOR

Bestselling author J. H. Croix lives in a small town in the historical farmlands of Maine with her husband and two spoiled dogs. Croix writes steamy contemporary romance with sassy independent women and rugged alpha men who aren't afraid to show some emotion. Her love for quirky small-towns and the characters that inhabit them shines through in her writing. Take a walk on the wild side of romance with her bestselling novels!

Places you can find me:
jhcroixauthor.com
jhcroix@jhcroix.com

www.ingramcontent.com/pod-product-compliance
Lightning Source LLC
Chambersburg PA
CBHW050516190726
48284CB00003B/822